# Snowbound

# Snowbound
## Ann M. Martin

AN
**APPLE**
PAPERBACK

SCHOLASTIC INC.
New York Toronto London Auckland Sydney

*This special book is for*
*a very special person,*
*Nikki Vach.*

Cover art by Hodges Soileau

Interior illustrations
by Angelo Tillery

ISBN 0-590-44963-X

12 11 10 9 8 7 6 5 4 3 2 1                    1 2 3 4 5 6/9

Printed in the U.S.A.                              40

First Scholastic printing, December 1991

★ ★ ★ ★

# THE STONEYBROOK NEWS

$1.00                                                    December

# BLIZZARD

## 23 INCHES OF SNOW !

## WIND CHILL   MINUS  8°

Ms. Kristy Thomas
1210 McLelland Road
Stoneybrook, CT 06800


Ms. Marian Tan, Editor
The Stoneybrook News
One Stoneybrook Plaza
Stoneybrook, CT 06800


Dear Mrs. Tan:

Hi! My name is Kristy Thomas. (Well, I guess you already knew that from the return address.) I am thirteen years old and I'm an eighth-grader at Stoneybrook Middle School. I am writing you to find out if you're interested in an article on that blizzard we had last week. The article you published in your newspaper after the storm was very informative, but it didn't tell what happened to people during the blizzard. My friends and I had lots of adventures and different experiences. One of my friends even got stranded in a car and almost froze to death! Some funny things happened, too. My friends and I are very close, and we share our lives with each other. So after the blizzard, we each wrote down

1

how we weathered the storm. Get it? WEATHERed the STORM? Anyway, then we passed our stories around so we could read them. The stories are fascinating (really-- I'm not bragging), so I thought other people might want to read them, too.

If you would like to print a young people's account of the blizzard, just let me know. I will be happy to edit my friends' stories and make them into an article. It can be however long you want.

I won't hold any rights to the story, but I would appreciate it if you would print "By Kristy Thomas" under the big headline that reads "SNOWBOUND!"

Yours sincerely,
Kristy Thomas


P.S. If you want to pay me, I wouldn't mind. How much do reporters earn? (I won't be too picky.)
P.P.S. Do you have any children? If so, I know a good baby-
sitting ser—

"**K**risty, erase that!"

"What?"

"Erase that P.P.S. This is a letter about a newspaper article, not the Baby-sitters Club."

My best friend, Mary Anne Spier, is far too practical. I didn't think an announcement about our business could hurt anything. Even so, I took out the P.P.S. It wasn't worth arguing over.

Boy, you will never believe what happened to me and my friends in the Baby-sitters Club (BSC) when a huge blizzard hit our little town of Stoneybrook, Connecticut, last week. The storm caught everyone by surprise, and different things happened to all of us. Some of our adventures were scary, some were exciting . . . and mine was funny! Most of us were separated during the storm. We were also out of touch, because after awhile, the phone lines went down. (Also, the power went out.) So we didn't hear about the adventures until the next day, when we could gab on the phone again.

Considering how fascinating our experiences were, I was surprised to read the article headed "Blizzard" in the paper the next day. I know I told the editor, Marian Tan, that the article was very informative (and it was), but the truth is, it was also an incredible bore. It mentioned lots of facts and statistics. For instance, about 28" of snow fell in Stoneybrook, and there was this wind chill factor of minus 8 degrees. But the article didn't say anything about *people*. There was no human interest. What about the cars that got stranded (I mean, with people in them)? What about parents who had left their kids with baby-sitters and couldn't get home to them? And what about people who got stuck at airports?

I decided that my article would give people the kind of news they wanted. Interesting news. If only Marian Tan would print it.

"Mary Anne?" I said. "How long do you think we'll have to wait to hear from the editor?" (I am not the most patient person in the world.)

"I don't know," she answered. "In the meantime, let's go over the material you've collected."

# Kristy

Sunday

Sunday was a pretty regular weekend day. Homework. Spending time with my family. Talking to Bart on the phone. Even the weather report was normal (but boring). The newscaster was predicting a snowstorm. Big woo. It was the fourth storm that had been predicted in two weeks and not a single flake of snow had fallen. I turned off the radio and went back to my homework. Here's how boring the snowstorm prediction was: my homework seemed fascinating in comparison....

"**K**risty, can you please help me with my sweater?"

I turned around. I was sitting at the desk in my room, slaving over a math problem. Since I was nowhere near solving it, I didn't mind the interruption. My stepsister, Karen, was standing in the doorway.

"For heaven's sake. Why are you wearing your sweater on your legs?" I asked. Karen had put each of her feet through a sleeve of her sweater and was now struggling to hold the bottom of the sweater around her waist.

"It's a new style," Karen replied. "Sweater-pants." She hobbled over to my desk. "Can you button me up the back, please?"

"I have a feeling," I said as I fastened the buttons, "that this isn't what Nannie had in mind when she knitted this sweater for you."

Nannie is my grandmother. She and Karen are just two of the people in my big, jumbly family. The others are my mom; my step-father, Watson; my three brothers (Charlie, who's seventeen; Sam, who's fifteen; and David Michael, who's seven); my stepbrother, Andrew (he's four and Karen is seven); and my adopted sister, Emily Michelle. Emily is two and a half. Mom and Watson adopted her from Vietnam. I don't really think of her as my *adopted* sister. She's just my sister, the same as Karen and Andrew are just my sister and brother.

That's a big family, right? Nannie is Mom's mother. She helps care for Emily while Mom and Watson are at work. Karen and Andrew are Watson's kids from his first marriage. Usually, they live with us every other weekend, but this December they were living with us for two weeks while their mom and stepfather went on a ski vacation. (Karen and Andrew's other house is right here in Stoneybrook, not far from their father's house.) They had arrived yesterday. When Karen is here, things are never dull.

Karen pranced out of my room, wearing her sweater-pants.

"What are you going to do now?" I asked her.

"Play with Emily Junior." (Emily is Karen's rat. Karen named her after Emily Michelle. I think that was a compliment.)

I turned back to my homework, but those numbers and signs sort of swam around on the paper. I let my mind wander. It wandered right to the Winter Wonderland Dance. It was going to be held on Friday evening after school, and it would be a pretty big deal. It was for every student at SMS — sixth-graders, seventh-graders, and eighth-graders. For once, every single one of my friends and I had a date for the dance. We planned to attend together, seven girls and seven boys. We couldn't wait. The decorating committee was going to transform the SMS gym into a snowy fairyland — sparkly flakes and white cotton-drifts, tinsel icicles. It would be awesome.

In the past, I have not thought much about dances, but now they're a little more meaningful. This is because I have a friend. I mean, a friend who's a boy. Oh, all right. He's my boyfriend. I guess. I never thought I would have a boyfriend. My friends say I'm a tomboy, and I suppose that's true. I love sports. I'm happiest wearing jeans and running shoes. Basically, I think makeup is a waste of time. And jewelry? I can take it or leave it. I don't even have pierced ears.

However, I met Bart.

Everything changed. No, that's not true. Bart and I met because we each coach a softball team for little kids. So our friendship is founded on sports. Also, I would still rather wear blue jeans than a dress. And I don't plan to get my ears pierced. But . . . I look forward to spending time with Bart. And I was particularly looking forward to going to the Winter Wonderland Dance with him. I was even look-

8

ing forward to wearing a dress (since I would only be in it for a few hours). Plus, going to a dance with all of my friends and all of their dates would be really fun. Mary Anne and I had been talking about the event for weeks. We planned to buy carnations for our dates. (We had a feeling they might be buying corsages for us.)

I could hear the phone ring then. It brought me back to reality, and I tried to focus on the math problem.

"Kris-teeee!" I heard David Michael call from the first floor. "Phone for you! It's your *boy-friend*. It's . . . *Bart, Bart bo Bart, banana fana fo —* "

I was at the top of the stairs before David Michael could sing another syllable of his stupid song. "Be *quiet!*" I hissed. "Do you want Bart to hear you?"

"Yes," replied David Michael. He started the song over.

I sprinted into Mom's room, grabbed the receiver off the phone, and began talking loudly, hoping Bart wouldn't hear my brother. At last David Michael whispered, "Cowabunga, dude," into the phone, and then (thankfully) hung up the extension.

"Sorry about that," I said to Bart.

"Who wound him up?" was Bart's reply.

9

"Oh, no one. It's Christmas, I think. Karen is loony, too."

"Actually, so's my little brother. Except he's loony because he *still* thinks we're going to get some snow."

I laughed. "The only snowflakes we're going to see will be decorating the walls of the gym for the dance on Friday. Oh, by the way," I went on, trying to sound nonchalant, "what color suit are you wearing?"

"Puce."

*Puce?* Where was I going to find a puce carnation? Even worse, my dress was red. We were going to clash horribly. See? That's the problem with dressing up. You have to worry about things like colors clashing. Or whether your slip will show. "Puce?" I repeated.

"Well, not really. I'm just teasing, Kristy. My suit is black."

That made life easier. Almost any color goes with black. Even gray. I almost giggled. I pictured myself in the flower store, asking the clerk for a gray carnation. I would tell him, "It's for an elephant."

Bart and I spoke for a few more minutes. We got off the phone when I heard Karen screaming from the playroom. I ran to her. "For heaven's sake, what's the matter?"

"Emily Junior is gone!" wailed Karen.

Sure enough, the rat cage was empty. Great. Mom and Nannie were going to love this. For that matter, Watson wouldn't be especially thrilled.

"What happened?" I asked. (I could hear the rest of my family making a dash for the playroom.)

"She's just gone," replied Karen. "Kidnapped, probably." (Karen has mysteries and detective stories on the brain.) "No sign of a struggle, though."

Guess what. My family searched high and low for Emily Junior that evening — and we didn't find her. Oh, goody. A rat was missing in our house. Now I could rest easy.

I returned to my room and the math problem. After I had stared at my paper for awhile and still had not figured out what to do next, I stood up, stretched, and switched on my stereo. I tuned the radio to WSTO, the Voice of Stoneybrook. Can you believe it? The weatherwoman (that's what *I* call her, even though the people on WSTO call her a weather*girl*) was predicting snow again. She said the storm would hit the next day.

What a laugh.

I turned off the radio. I finished my homework. Then I read a story to Andrew and David Michael. Andrew, thinking positively,

11

had requested that I read *Katy and the Big Snow*. So I did. Then I helped him get ready for bed. I was all set to *put* him to bed, too, but he asked for Daddy, so I called Watson upstairs.

I checked on Karen. She was crawling around on her hands and knees. I knew she was looking for Emily Junior again.

"Karen," I said, "I'm sure she'll turn up."

Karen got to her feet. "I guess," she replied.

"It's supposed to snow tomorrow," I told her, trying to cheer her up.

Karen transformed before my eyes. "It *is?*" (She never gets tired of hoping for snow.) "Oh, yippee, yippee, yippeeeee!" she screeched.

I returned to my room. I opened my closet and gazed for awhile at the red dress for the Winter Wonderland Dance.

That night, I dreamed of snowflakes and carnations and Bart. In the dream, a storm hit Stoneybrook. Only it snowed fat white carnations, which showered down on Bart and me.

# CHAPTER 2

# Claudia

monday

Heres how to descibe monday. Partly claudy and cold but not to cold. So where was our snow. Once again it didn't' arrive. This afternon I baby - sat for Myria and Gabie and Laura perkins. Mariah and Gabby were realy disapperntened about the snow. I mean the no snow. They have been waiting patently for a storm or even a flury.

*Claudia*

So I'm not a very good speller. So sue me.

Oops. Sorry. I know I sound defensive. My friend Stacey McGill tells me so. Kristy does, too, of course. If something is on her mind, she says it.

I'm Claudia Kishi. I'm one of the members of the Baby-sitters Club. In fact, I'm the vice-president. And I'm *not* a good speller, or even a very good student, but my friends don't care. (I wish my parents and teachers would follow their examples.)

Well, another snowy forecast, another wrong prediction. There was only one good thing about the lack of snow. I didn't have to worry whether the SMS Winter Wonderland Dance would be held. In past years, it has been canceled three times due to bad weather. And I wanted desperately to go. My date was going to be Iri Mitsuhashi, this kid who's in a couple of my classes. We aren't girlfriend-and-boyfriend or anything, but we are friends and we have fun together. In case you're wondering, Iri is Japanese. So am I. Well, we're Japanese-American. Our parents were born in Japan; we were born in America.

Here are the reasons I wanted snow:

I wanted school to be canceled. (I usually do.)

I wanted snow for Christmas.

The kids in Stoneybrook were getting zooey because practically every other day, snow was forecast — and then it didn't come. That Monday afternoon, the Perkins girls were pretty disappointed. And they weren't the only ones.

"The triplets are driving me crazy!" exploded Mallory Pike as she entered my room for that day's BSC meeting. "All they do is complain because they haven't been able to build a snow fort yet."

"Tell me about it," replied Jessi Ramsey. "Becca's been moping for days."

"Well, guess what I did," said Kristy. "Last night I told Karen we were supposed to have snow today. I told her because she was upset that Emily Junior is missing — "

"*She is?*" interrupted Mary Anne. "Remind me not to baby-sit at your house until . . . until the problem has been straightened out."

"So now," Kristy continued, "Emily is still missing *and* it didn't snow."

The time was 5:23, according to my digital clock (the official club timepiece). Three afternoons a week — Mondays, Wednesdays, and Fridays, from five-thirty until six — the members of the BSC hold a meeting. The members are Kristy Thomas, me, Stacey McGill, Mary

15

Anne Spier, Dawn Schafer, Mallory Pike, and Jessi Ramsey. What do we do at our meetings? We take phone calls from people in Stoneybrook who need sitters for their kids. My friends and I wind up with lots of jobs that way. Our club has become a real business. And we run it professionally.

Kristy is the president. The club was her idea. She figured out how to make it work, and she keeps the rest of us on our toes!

I'm the vice-president because the meetings are held in my room. They're held there because I'm the only one of us who has not only a private phone but a private phone number. This is important. We get a lot of calls during most of our meetings, and we'd hate to tie up some grown-up's phone three times a week.

Stacey McGill is our treasurer. She collects weekly dues and keeps track of the money we earn. She's also my best friend — the first best friend I've ever had. Stacey and I are alike in that we both adore wild clothes and wild jewelry, fixing our hair, painting our nails — that sort of thing. (I even have two holes pierced in one ear, and one hole in the other. Stacey just has one hole in each ear.) Sometimes, since I *love* art, I make jewelry for us. If I may be honest, I must add that Stacey and I (and this isn't bragging) are a little more sophisticated than the other club members — even Dawn, Mary Anne, and Kristy, who are thirteen-year-old SMS eighth-graders, just like Stacey and me. (Jessi and Mal are eleven and in sixth grade at SMS.) Stacey and I have really different lives, though. Stacey's parents are divorced, and she's an only child. My parents are not divorced, and I have an older sister, Janine. Stacey grew up in New York City. I grew up here in Stoneybrook. (Stacey still visits New York pretty often, though, because her dad lives there.) One other difference: Stacey has a disease called diabetes. I don't understand the technical stuff about her illness, but I do know that she has to be very careful about what she eats because her body doesn't break down blood sugar properly. Too much or too little sugar and she can get *really* sick. (Stacey has a severe form of the disease. She's called a brittle diabetic.) Every day, she has to test her blood, count calories, pay strict attention to her diet (no candy or gooey desserts, which would be a real trial for me, since I'm a junk-food addict), and give herself injections of this stuff called insulin. (The idea of giving myself a shot grosses me out, but not Stacey. She's used to it.)

The club secretary is Mary Anne Spier. Her job is to maintain the BSC record book — keep

17

it up-to-date and accurate. To do that, Mary Anne has to know the complicated schedules of the seven club members. Then, when someone calls needing a baby-sitter, Mary Anne can check the appointment pages in the book and see who's free to take the job. Being the secretary isn't easy, but Mary Anne is a very careful worker.

Mary Anne is Kristy's best friend, but she sure is different from her. She's shy, she's softspoken, she cries easily — and she has a steady boyfriend! His name is Logan Bruno. (Of course, Logan and Mary Anne were going to go to the Winter Wonderland Dance together.) Mary Anne grew up with just her dad. She had no brothers or sisters, and her mom died when Mary Anne was a baby. But things have changed. Mr. Spier recently remarried. And guess who his new wife is — Dawn Schafer's mother. So now Mary Anne and Dawn are stepsisters *and* best friends. (Mary Anne is lucky. She has two best friends.) Mary Anne, Dawn, and their dad and mom live in this wonderful old farmhouse that Mrs. Schafer bought.

Dawn is the alternate officer of the BSC. This means she can fill in for any other officer if that person has to miss a meeting for some reason. Dawn has to know everything — how to schedule appointments, how to keep track of the money in the treasury, etc. Her job is not simple, but since club members rarely miss meetings, she doesn't have to take over very often.

You might be wondering how Dawn's mom and Mary Anne's dad got together. This is an interesting story. Both Mr. Spier and Mrs. Schafer grew up in Stoneybrook. They were sweethearts in high school, but they lost track of each other when Mrs. Schafer left for college in California. While she was on the West Coast, she met Mr. Schafer and got married, and they had Dawn and Dawn's younger brother, Jeff. When Dawn was twelve, though, her parents decided to divorce, so Mrs. Schafer moved back to Stoneybrook with Dawn and Jeff. She met up with Mr. Spier again (who was Mary Anne's father by then) and they got married the following year. That's when Mary Anne and Dawn became stepsisters. Now the Spiers and Schafers are one big happy family — most of the time. They've had their share of problems. I guess the worst was that Jeff never grew to like Stoneybrook. He just wasn't happy here. So he returned to California to live with his dad. Dawn and Jeff get to see each other pretty often, though. They fly across the country a lot, and they run up *huge* phone bills!

Our California girl is beautiful. Her hair is long and shiny and so blonde it's practically white. Her eyes are blue and she looks . . . healthy. I'm not sure how to describe that. Glowing, maybe? Anyway, this might be a result of the tons of health food Dawn consumes. She's as addicted to raw vegetables and tofu as I am to Ring-Dings and Devil Dogs. We could never live together, but I think Stacey enjoys having Dawn around because the two of them can turn down my goodies and pig out on whatever appeals to them — pretzels, crackers, stuff without sugar. *Blech.* I love Dawn despite this flaw, though. She's an individual, sure of herself (mostly), happy to go her own way, dress her own way, make her own friends. Everyone is glad Dawn came to Connecticut and joined the club.

Jessi Ramsey and Mal Pike (their names are shortened versions of Jessica and Mallory) are the BSC's junior officers. They don't have actual club duties. "Junior officer" means that since they're younger than the rest of us, they aren't allowed to baby-sit at night, unless they're taking care of their own brothers and sisters. They are a huge help, anyway. Since they take over a lot of the afternoon and weekend jobs, they free up us older sitters for the evenings.

Like Stacey and me, Mal and Jessi are best friends. Their lives are similar in many ways. They're both the oldest kids in their families; they feel that, despite this, their parents still treat them like babies; and they have a passion for reading, especially horse stories and mysteries. There are some differences, too, of course. While Jessi has one younger sister and a baby brother, Mal has *seven* younger sisters and brothers. Three of them are ten-year-old identical triplets (Byron, Jordan, and Adam). Then there're Vanessa, Nicky, Margo, and Claire. Claire is the baby. Well, she's five, but she's the youngest in the family. Mal and Jessi may love reading, but Jessi's true interest is ballet, and Mal's is writing. You should see Jessi dance. (I have.) She's incredible. She takes lessons at a special dance school in Stamford, a city not far from Stoneybrook. She had to audition just to be able to take lessons there. And she's danced the lead role in several productions, performing onstage before hundreds of people. Mal, on the other hand, hopes to be an author one day. She likes to draw, too, so she thinks she might become a children's author and illustrator. Guess what.

Even though they're only eleven, Mal and Jessi both have semiboyfriends who are taking them to the Winter Wonderland Dance. Mal's is Ben Hobart. He's new at SMS and he's Australian! (He and his family live across the street from me, next to the Perkinses.) Jessi's is Quint Walter. She met him in New York City, which is where he lives. Quint is a ballet dancer, too, and attends a special performing arts school. Jessi and Quint have not seen each other since Jessi's trip to the city — but in just two days, Quint will be traveling to Stoney-brook to stay with the Ramseys and go to the dance. As you can imagine, Mal and Jessi are nearly hysterical with excitement over the dance. Let me see. Oh yes. One other thing — Mal is white and Jessi is black.

"You guys? Hey, guys, we have a lot to talk about. . . . Guys?"

That was Kristy. She had called the club meeting to order about six times, and the rest of us were still jabbering away.

"Hey, I was thinking!" shouted Kristy. "We might as well cancel our next meeting. So many of us are going to be busy on Wednesday." That got our attention. Club meetings are rarely canceled.

"Mal and I will be baby-sitting," spoke up Mary Anne. "That's the marathon when Mr. and Mrs. Pike go to New York for a day and won't be home until, like one in the morning or something. I'm spending the night at Mal's." (The Pikes have so many kids that the children require *two* baby-sitters.) "Who else is busy?"

"I am," replied Jessi. "Rehearsal for *The Nutcracker*."

"I might be, remember?" added Dawn. "Jeff's coming home for Christmas sometime that evening. I'm not sure when Mom and I will be leaving to pick him up at the airport."

"I'm baby-sitting for the Perkins girls again on Wednesday evening," I said, "but I'll be around in the afternoon. Why don't I stay here and take phone messages? I don't mind."

We decided that was a good idea. Then we spent the rest of the meeting answering job calls, scheduling appointments, and talking about the dance. I have to admit that the dance was a pretty big deal. For instance, Kristy had invited Bart, who doesn't attend our school, and Jessi was going to introduce Quint to the kids of SMS. An out-of-town boyfriend was quite special. Futhermore, I don't know about anyone else, but *I* was really looking forward to dressing up. I'd bought this black velvet knicker outfit and was going to wear it with a lot of silver jewelry, including snowflake earrings. Now, if only the weather would cool off and it would snow for real.

# CHAPTER 3

## Dawn

Monday

I was sorry we had to cancel a club meeting, that's for sure, but I couldn't wait to see Jeff on Wednesday. It seemed as if years had passed since we were last together. (Actually, it was only a few weeks.) I wouldn't even mind the boring car ride to the airport, since when we got there, Mom and I would soon be reunited with Jeff. Mary Anne, I wish you could have come with us, but you were on your baby-sitting marathon. Oh, well. You would see Jeff Thursday morning.

## Dawn

"Good-bye!"

" 'Bye, you guys!"

"See you tomorrow!"

"Don't forget — no Wednesday meeting!"

Our Monday BSC meeting was breaking up. It was Claud who'd reminded us that the next meeting had been canceled.

And it was Mary Anne who said, "Wait a sec! The dance!"

"What about it?" I asked.

"The dance is Friday evening. If we skip our Wednesday meeting, the next meeting should be on Friday, but can we hold a meeting right before the dance?"

"Well, we better not cancel two meetings in a row," said Kristy. "Don't worry. We'll figure out something. See you guys in school tomorrow!"

We weren't worried. We were too wound up to be worried. So much was going on. Jeff was arriving, Mary Anne's big Pike job was coming up, Christmas was approaching, and then there was the dance, of course. I was going to go with Price Irving, this guy at school. He wasn't new or anything, but I hadn't noticed him until a few weeks ago. Overnight, I had developed this amazing crush on him. And then he had invited me to go to the dance with him. The weird thing is that I had just gotten up the nerve to invite *him*, and the very next day I was dashing through the halls at school, trying to get from one class to another without killing myself as I dodged through the crowd of kids, when I executed one good dodge — only to run directly into Price.

I almost said, "Oh, my lord," which is what Claudia would have said, but I caught myself in time and simply said, "Sorry." (Meanwhile, this little voice in my brain was chanting, "You are such a jerk, you are such a jerk.") How could I ask him out *now*?

Price solved the problem for me. He grinned. "That's okay," he replied. "I'm glad you ran into me." (I laughed.) "I wanted to ask you something. Um, Dawn, um, Dawn, um — "

"Yeah?" I prompted him.

After about half an hour (well, not really), Price managed to invite me to the dance. Of course I accepted. I'm no fool. And now the dance was just four days away, and I had bought a new dress and everything.

Life was good.

"Excited, sweetie?" Mom asked me after supper that night.

"Very. It's going to be dreamy," I said, and sighed.

Mom frowned. "Dreamy?"

"Yeah. He's so . . . incredible."

"Incredible? Jeff?"

"No, Price," I said.

Mom laughed. "I meant, are you excited about Jeff's visit?"

"Oh! I thought you were asking about the dance. Yeah. Of course I'm excited. I can't wait to see Jeff. Dad, too."

My winter vacation was going to be busy. Jeff would stay with us until the day after Christmas, and then he *and I* were going to fly back to California and I would visit with Dad and Jeff until New Year's Day.

"Hey, can I call Jeff?" I asked Mom. I looked at my watch. "It's five o'clock out there. This is probably a good time to reach him."

"Sure, sweetie," said Mom. "Go ahead. Ask him about his flight while you're at it."

I dialed California. The phone rang twice before someone picked it up. "Simpson's Clothing Boutique. Bra department," said a voice.

"Jeff!" I exclaimed.

"Uh-oh. Dawn?"

"Yeah."

"I thought you were going to be Oliver."

I giggled. "Anyway, hi. Can you talk for a minute? Mom said I could call you. Is this a good time?"

"Sure. It's fine."

"I'm sorry I'm not Oliver. I just wanted to ask you about Wednesday. You're still on the same flight?"

"Yup." Jeff paused. "It stops in Chicago, though."

"I know. But it just stops, right? You don't have to change planes or anything, do you?" Not that it would matter. Jeff is a champion flyer.

"Nope. Just a stop."

"Do you have enough stuff to do on the plane?"

"Yup."

"Jeff, is anything wrong?" My brother may not be a big talker, but usually he can do better than this.

"Well, I was thinking. What if we were flying along and suddenly the plane lost its engine power and we crashed? What if we flew right into a mountain like those people did in that movie?"

"That isn't going to happen," I said.

"How do you know?"

"I don't. . . . But we've both flown lots of times, and the worst flight we ever had was that really, really bumpy one."

"Yeah. You never know, though."

My stomach began to feel funny. "Jeff, you are coming, aren't you?" I asked.

"I wish I didn't have to fly," was his answer.

"Oh, Jeff, please! It's Christmas. We're waiting until you come before we decorate the tree. Don't stay in California. You *have* to come." Even as the words were leaving my mouth, I knew I'd said the wrong thing.

"I do not *have* to come," replied Jeff.

"No. No, you don't. I didn't mean that. I'm just looking forward to your visit."

"But what if the plane *does* crash?"

"What if it doesn't and you stay in California and miss a wonderful trip to see Mom and me?"

"At least I'll be alive."

I sighed.

When Jeff and I hung up, I told Mom about our conversation.

Mom frowned slightly, but she said, "Don't worry. Jeff will be all right. I think he's going through a phase." (This is a very parent thing to say. According to adults, kids are always going through phases.) "Jeff's reacting to the divorce," Mom went on. (Oh, divorce fallout.)

"He's having a little trouble with separation. He'll be okay once he gets here."

I nodded. "In two days the flight will be over. Then Jeff can relax." So could I. I would feel better when he was actually in our house.

While Mary Anne and I were getting ready for bed that night, we tuned into WSTO on the radio. "Hey, listen," said Mary Anne, putting down her hairbrush.

"Snow is on the way, folks!" the weather forecaster was saying. "Heavy accumulations expected on Wednesday."

"Yeah, right," I said, and shook my head.

# CHAPTER 4

## Mallory

Tuesday

Yes! Mom and Dad were going to leave for New York EARLY the next morning. Then Mary Anne and I would be in charge for almost 24 hours! Mary Anne was going to spend TWO nights at my house, starting that night. (That was so she wouldn't have to come over at the crack of dawn in the morning, when my parents left for the train.) It was going to be one of the biggest, most important baby-sitting jobs ever. Mom and Dad wouldn't be back until after MIDNIGHT!

Mallory
☺

When Mom and Dad first started talking about this trip to New York, some teensy little part of my brain hoped I might be left in charge (well, accompanied by another baby-sitter, since that's the Pike rule). Then I found out that my parents were going to leave extra early in the morning and not return until, like, two A.M.

I lost all hope.

But *then* Mom and Dad said that if an older sitter (like thirteen is *so* much older than eleven) would spend Tuesday and Wednesday nights at our house, they would consider letting me take on half the job. (The holiday spirit must have been getting the better of them.) As it turned out, Mary Anne was able to do the job with me. I couldn't believe her father would allow her to sleep over at someone's house for two nights in a row during school. But he did. (The holiday spirit must have been getting to him, too. Our parents were acting so . . . sane.)

"So what are you going to do on your trip to the Big Apple?" I asked Mom one day. I myself have been to New York several times.

"Lots of things," Mom replied. "Your dad and I have planned quite a day. We're going

33

to eat a light breakfast at the Embassy — "

"That *coffee* shop?" I exclaimed. I would have chosen the Plaza or some place.

"I love coffee shops!" Mom replied. "Besides, we'll eat lunch and dinner at fancier places. Anyway, after breakfast we're going to go to the Metropolitan Museum of Art. Then we'll take a bus across Central Park and go to the Museum of Natural History. Then we'll head downtown and go shopping. Everything will look so pretty for the holidays! Your dad and I will have to take you kids there one December. Maybe next year. You'd love the decorations. A giant shimmery snowflake is suspended over Fifth Avenue. At Rockefeller Center is the biggest Christmas tree you can imagine, and it's covered with tiny lights. And the windows of Saks — "

"Mom, Mom, I can't stand it," I interrupted. "Can't I go with you?"

"Sorry, honey," replied my mother. "Let's see. We're meeting the Sombergs for lunch and the four of us decided to try a new restaurant. In the afternoon, your dad and I plan to visit the Museum of Broadcasting and maybe walk around Lincoln Center. Then we're going to meet the Wileys for dinner, and after *that* we're going to see *The Phantom of the Opera*. Then we'll come home."

34

"Wow," said Claire, who'd been listening. "Will you ever get to go to the bathroom?"

Leave it to Claire to make a connection between New York City and the bathroom.

Mary Anne came over after dinner on Tuesday evening.

"Are you ready for two nights and a day at the Pike Zoo?" I asked her.

"Hey, no problem," Mary Anne replied. "I'm a pro at this."

That was true. Mary Anne has come along as a mother's helper on a couple of Pike vacations. She can survive us for weeks at a time.

Mary Anne stepped into our house and set her duffel bag on the floor. She called good-bye to her father, who had walked her over.

"Hello, Mary Anne-silly-billy-goo-goo!" cried Claire, running downstairs and wrapping her arms around Mary Anne's legs. "Silly-billy-goo-goo" is a term Claire attaches to names of people she likes — when she's in her silly mood, which is fairly often.

Claire was followed by our brother Nicky, who's eight. "Crumble!" ordered Nicky, and Claire let go of Mary Anne and dropped to her hands and knees, tucking her head to her chest.

35

"What are they doing?" Mary Anne whispered to me.

"Nicky told Claire he has a special power over her," I whispered back. "Anytime he tells her to crumble, she has to hit the floor, no matter where she is or what she's doing. Nicky says he'll have this power forever, and that years from now, at Claire's wedding, he's going to wait until she's walking down the aisle and then he's going to whisper 'Crumble' to her."

Mary Anne smiled. But she didn't say anything about our family being a zoo until the triplets bounded down the stairs, pointing their fingers at Nicky and going, "Bzzzz!"

"Not the Bizzer Sign," I muttered. I thought my brothers had forgotten about that. The Bizzer Sign is this annoying insult thing. They used to give each other the sign all the time. It never failed to get a rise out of the younger kids. Sure enough, Nicky turned to me with a pained expression and whined, "They're giving me the *Bizzer* Sign."

"Good," said Claire. "My crumble is over then."

"Is not!" cried Nicky.

"Is too!"

"Kids!" called Mom from the living room. "What's going on?"

"Nothing!" chorused Claire, Nicky, Byron, Adam, and Jordan. They turned and fled upstairs.

"Nice move," I said to Mom. I led Mary Anne into the living room. "Here's Mary Anne," I added unnecessarily.

Mom and Dad were reading the newspaper. They smiled as we plopped onto the couch.

It was time for . . . the Briefing. Mom and Dad were going to talk to us about our baby-sitting job. Dad had written out a sheet of instructions, reminders, notes, phone numbers, and addresses. He handed it to Mary Anne and me. Even so, Mary Anne pulled a pen and a small notepad out of her purse and sat poised to take notes. (She is *such* a good secretary.)

"Let's see," Mom began. "First of all, Mary Anne, you'll be sharing Mal and Vanessa's room. We'll set up a cot for you in there."

"We'd give you our room," added Dad, "but we'll be using it tonight, as well as after we come home tomorrow. You two really don't have much of a nighttime job. Mrs. Pike and I will be gone for less than twenty-four hours."

"Yeah. All we have to do is watch seven kids for the entire day," I said.

"They'll be in school for six hours," Mom pointed out.

"That's true."

"Anyway, Mallory," Mom continued, "Dad and I plan to get up at five tomorrow, drive to the station, and catch the six-thirty train. We're going to be hard to reach while we're gone, but if there's a real emergency, you can call the Sombergs or the Wileys and they'll give us a message when they see us."

"Their phone numbers are on the sheet I gave you," said Dad.

"Also," Mom went on, "several of the neighbors know we're going to be gone tomorrow. So if you need help, you could call Mrs. McGill or Mrs. Barrett or the Braddocks — "

"Or my dad," added Mary Anne. "He'll be home tomorrow night."

"Great," said Mom. "Now about meals — I desperately need to go to the grocery, but you have enough food for tomorrow. There's cereal and fruit for breakfast and the fixings for sloppy joes for dinner. I'll leave enough cash so you can buy your lunches at school tomorrow and Thursday. There should also be enough food for Thursday morning breakfast, and then I'll go to the grocery as soon I can that morning."

Mary Anne was taking down practically every word my parents said. She had filled three pages on her little pad and had just started a fourth. (She is a teensy bit compulsive.)

"So," I said to Mom and Dad, "how much money are you going to leave us? Not that we'll need it for anything except school lunches, but you never know."

Mom forked over a roll of bills. "I expect to get most of this back," she said.

I looked at the fortune in my hands. "Where am I going to keep this? We better have a good hiding place." I gave the money to Mary Anne. "Here, you hide it," I said. "I can't do it. I'm afraid I'll lose it."

Mary Anne took the money, Mom and Dad gave us a few more instructions, and then Mom said, "I think I'll go upstairs and have a talk with the triplets about the Bizzer Sign."

"I'll help you two set up the cot," said Dad to Mary Anne and me.

"Oh, we can do it!" I cried. "Come on, Mary Anne."

Mary Anne and I were busily wedging the cot between Vanessa's bed and mine,

41

when Adam charged into the room.

"Don't bother knocking," said Vanessa, who was seated at her desk. She frowned, then added, "And please stop your mocking." (Vanessa plans to be a poetess.)

"I didn't say anything!" exclaimed Adam. "Yet."

"What's up?" I asked. I thought maybe he was going to complain because Mom had talked to him and Byron and Jordan about the Bizzer Sign.

Adam grinned broadly. "Guess what I just heard on the news," he said. Then he added meaningfully, "On WSTO."

I glanced at Mary Anne and shrugged.

Vanessa looked up long enough to say, "A war? A robber? A traffic jam? A prisoner is on the lam?"

Adam made a face. "*No!* The weather guy just said we're supposed to get a big snowstorm tomorrow."

What on old, tired story. I put a striped case on a pillow and arranged the pillow on Mary Anne's cot.

"Hey, Vanessa," Adam went on, "you can put away your homework. We won't be having any school tomorrow."

"Have you done yours yet?" Mary Anne

asked Adam. "Because I sure wouldn't count on a snow day."

"Most of it," Adam muttered. He left the room, looking gloomy.

But I felt great.

I caught Mary Anne's eye. Our adventure was about to begin!

# CHAPTER 5

## Stacey

Wednesday

Yea! No snow, no snow, no snow! I know most kids (probably most adults, too) start praying for snow the second a weather forecaster so much as says the word. But snow was the last thing I wanted on Wednesday, and since it had been predicted (again), I was pretty happy when, by the end of school that day, we were still snow-free. I could not wait to get home and bug Mom.

Mom had made a major promise. She had said I could get my hair permed for the Winter Wonderland Dance. It wouldn't be my first perm or anything, but I wanted a new one very badly. My old one looked kind of limp. It also looked like a perm. You want to know a beauty secret? Okay. The secret to good makeup and a good hair treatment is to look as if you have *no* makeup and *no* treatment. It's kind of odd to spend money on supplies and stuff when your goal is to look like you don't use them, but I guess the idea is to appear natural. Anyway, I needed a perm so I could look like I didn't have one.

I was going to the dance with this guy named Austin Bentley. I've been out with him before and so has Claudia. We don't love him. He's just a nice guy. So I invited him to the dance. Even if he wasn't a *special* date, I wanted to look good on Friday. Getting my hair permed was critical. So was going to Washington Mall.

Washington Mall is one of those huge shopping complexes that looks as if it had been dropped out of the sky and just happened to land in a parking lot by a major highway. It's enormous. In the mall are stores, restaurants, even a movie theater. Unfortunately, the mall is not in Stoneybrook. You have to drive, like, half an hour to get there, if you take the highway. If you take the back roads, the trip could be a lot longer.

Now, my mom is great, but one of her flaws is: She's afraid to drive in snow. She had said we could go to the mall for my perm *if* the roads were clear. The night before, when I'd heard the most recent WSTO weather forecast, I had panicked. Snow for Wednesday! No way Mom would drive me to the mall if a storm came. I'd have to settle on going to the local place on Thursday. And the local hair place, Gloriana's House of Hair, is not wonderful. (You should have seen what Gloriana did to Kristy's stepsister once.)

Can you understand why I was jubilant when I left school on Wednesday and *no snow* was falling? The sky was overcast, almost leaden, and the temperature had dropped to 28 degrees, but — no snow! (The weather was stuck in a rut.)

"Mom, Mom!" I called as soon as I ran in the door after school.

"In the kitchen, honey," she replied.

I found my mother seated at the kitchen table, paying bills. "It's not snowing," I announced.

Mom smiled. "You don't want to drive all the way out to the mall, do you?"

"Yes!" I cried. "I do! You said we could if — " I realized Mom was teasing. "So we're still going?" I asked.

"Sure," replied my mother. She glanced outside. "I don't see why not."

"Oh, thank you, thank you! Can Claudia come with us?"

"Of course."

"Yes!" I exclaimed. I made a grab for the phone and dialed Claudia's personal number. (She is so lucky.) "Hi," I said when Claudia answered. "It's me. We're still going to the mall. Want to come with us?"

"I do," replied Claudia, "but I better not. I don't think you'll be back in time. I'm sitting for the Perkinses tonight. And before that, I have to take BSC phone calls, since we're not holding our meeting. Remember? I promised Kristy. She'd kill me if I skipped out to go to the mall instead."

"Yeah. Sorry. I forgot that you volunteered to take calls. Can I get you anything from the mall?" (This was a dangerous question.)

"Just go drool over the stuff in the jewelry store, okay?"

I laughed. "Okay. Have fun at the Perkinses'. Call me when you get home."

"Okay," replied Claud. "See you."

I hung up the phone and immediately Mom pounced on me. "Stacey? You better eat something before we leave." (Like you can't buy food at the mall.) "And have you given yourself your insulin?"

For heaven's sake. I am thirteen. I have been taking care of my diabetes forever now. (Well, for a couple of years.) But I understood Mom's concern. Awhile ago, I *wasn't* careful about my diet — and I landed in the hospital.

"I won't need another injection for a couple of hours," I told Mom. "But I do need a snack. I'll eat it in the car, though."

"Are you in a hurry?" teased Mom.

I laughed. "Come *on*. I want to get going."

I put an apple, some carrot sticks, and a handful of wheat crackers in a bag. Then I herded Mom out to the car.

As we sped along the highway, I ate the apple and most of the crackers. I put the bag away and slid a cassette into the tape player.

The music came on.

I slid my eyes sideways, glancing at Mom. She was glancing at me.

"How come," I said, "this tape from a case labeled *Shout It!* by the Tin Can Voices is playing Vivaldi's *Four Seasons*?"

Mom raised her eyebrows. "Stacey, I'm impressed. You can recognize Vivaldi. I'll have to switch tapes more often."

"I suppose," I said, "that I'll find *Shout It!* in a Vivaldi case at home?"

"I wouldn't be surprised."

"Mom, this is cruelty to children," I protested. (We were laughing.)

I let Vivaldi play away. (Of course, Vivaldi him*self* wasn't playing. Vivaldi composed the music, but he's been dead for years.)

"Stacey, are you dressed warmly enough?" asked Mom out of the blue.

"You mean, considering the heater is blasting and the windows are rolled up?" I replied. (The truth is, I *wasn't* dressed warmly enough for a 28-degree day. But I was overdressed for equatorial weather, which was how the inside of the car felt. Mom doesn't have a very good heater control.)

"Stacey," said my mother warningly.

I knew that if I uttered one more word, she would say something like, "How badly do you want to go to the mall? Because we can always turn around and head right back home."

"Sorry," I apologized. "Okay. I'm not dressed *quite* warmly enough, but hey, I look good. Besides," I added quickly, seeing the expression on Mom's face, "we're hardly going to be outside at all. We just have to walk from the car into the mall and back. I can handle that."

Mom sighed. "I'm sure," she said, "that I never acted *any*thing like you when *I* was thirteen years old."

I leaned over and gave Mom a kiss on the cheek. "I love you," I said.

"I love you, too."

Washington Mall was, as Mom said, decorated to the teeth. For Christmas and Hanukkah, that is. She meant that it was overdecorated, both inside and out. The first thing I noticed as we approached the mall from the highway was this enormous neon Santa, a sleigh, eight reindeer, and Rudolph, perched atop Sears. Not far away, running across the outside of another department store, was a menorah outlined in lightbulbs. And tinsel was everywhere in the mall. It looked like an aluminum-foil factory had exploded.

We went inside. Not an inch of space was left undecorated. And in the center of the mall was a large gingerbread house, circled by a line of impatient children waiting to visit Santa Claus, who sat on a throne inside.

"Mommy, Mommy, can I go see Santa?" I asked.

Mom smiled. "Maybe next year, dear," she replied. "Come along."

We reached the beauty salon and luckily, Joyce, my favorite hairstylist, was free. Before long I was sitting in a chair, smelling like rotten eggs.

"Stace?" said Mom, who looked bored. "I'm going to run to Sears. I'll be back in a little while."

"Okay," I replied.

Joyce was hard at work. After awhile, I was ready to "cook" under the hair dryer. Then Joyce unwound my rollers. Mom returned. She watched as Joyce combed my hair out.

"You look great, honey," said Mom.

"Thanks! And thank you for letting me have the perm. I really appreciate it. I hope you know that."

We were standing at the counter, and Mom was writing out a check, when another client entered the salon. "Whew! It's really snowing!" she exclaimed.

I glanced at my mother. "Uh-oh," I said.

# CHAPTER 6

## Kristy

Wednesday

I hardly ever see Bart during the week, just for fun. Sometimes I see him at softball practices or games, but thats about it. Movies or anything spur-of-the-moment are reserved for weekends. But Wednesday was an exception, and I decided to make the most of it. Unfortunately, so did my little brothers and sisters.

It never occurred to me that a snowstorm would actually hit on Wednesday. If that had occurred to me, would I have invited Bart over? I have no idea.

Wednesday afternoon seemed strange. Well, it *was* a little strange. Unusual, anyway. Christmas was drawing near, so our house was decorated. Almost. Watson had strung lights on the fir tree in the front yard. Inside, evergreen branches were everywhere, along with our favorite old decorations. The only thing missing was the indoor tree. (We'd bought one; we just hadn't put it in the living room yet.) Also, as I mentioned before, Karen and Andrew were living with us for two weeks.

Most unusual, though, was . . . no BSC meeting. We've missed meetings here and there, but usually because my friends and I were on vacation. Or because we were all busy with some school event or project. But that day was just a semiregular Wednesday. I wondered what to do with myself. I had no sitting job and wasn't even needed to watch my younger brothers and sisters. So I got out my schoolbooks and did my homework. I finished early. Now what? An unexpected stretch of time lay before me.

The phone rang.

Bart! I thought, and dashed into the kitchen.

But the call was for Karen. Her friend Nancy wanted to know if Emily Junior had turned up. Very sadly, Karen admitted that she hadn't. When Karen got off the phone, I decided to call Bart myself.

Wait! What was I going to say to him?

In an instant, one of my brilliant ideas slipped into my brain. If it was okay with Mom and Nannie and Watson, I would invite Bart over to watch a couple of videos, and then maybe he could stay for dinner.

I was in luck. I got permission, *and* Charlie volunteered to drive me to the video store so I could rent some tapes.

I called Bart. "Want to come over?" I asked. "I thought we could watch some movies. And Mom said you can stay for dinner."

"To*day?*" replied Bart.

"Yeah."

"But it's Wednesday. It's a school day. And you have a BSC meeting." Bart sounded horribly confused.

"There's no meeting," I told him. "It was canceled. And you don't have to stay too late. Come on. It'll be fun. What movies do you feel like seeing?"

"Oh, funny ones."

Of *course* Bart seemed confused. We'd been spending more time together recently, but mostly on the weekends. I hardly ever called him on an afternoon in the middle of the week.

And I had certainly never invited him to dinner. To be honest, I was slightly nervous about exposing him to my family, but I thought it might be time to do that. I mean, Bart's met everyone from Nannie to Emily Michelle; he's just never had a dose of the *entire* Brewer/Thomas household for any period of time.

I hoped he liked rats.

"Do you mind if Emily Junior is on the loose?" I asked.

Not surprisingly, Bart sounded taken aback. Still, he said, "Nope."

"Good. I'll call you when I get back from the video store."

Ah. This seemed the perfect way to spend a cold, cloudy almost-winter afternoon. Movies, dinner, Bart.

Charlie drove me to the video store, and after hemming and hawing so long that my brother said, "Were you hoping to rent something before Christmas?" I finally chose two movies: *Uncle Buck* and *Back to the Future*.

I called Bart as soon as I was at home again. "Come on over," I said.

Then I set the movies on top of the television in the den. It was at this point that I noticed something disturbing. Karen, Andrew, David Michael, and Emily Michelle were not *doing* anything. They were hanging around the house, draping themselves across couches and chairs, whining, complaining, and occasionally yelling at one another.

They were bored.

"Nannie," I said nervously, "the kids are bored."

Nannie sighed. "Well . . ." Her voice trailed off.

"Oh, please. I don't want them pestering us when — "

*Ding-dong.*

" — Bart is here," I finished.

And at that moment, eight little feet thundered toward the front door.

"I'll get it!" I screeched.

I ran for the door and edged the kids away.

"Who is it?" asked David Michael. "Is it your . . . boyfriend?"

My hand was on the door. I was all set to open it for Bart, who was probably freezing. Instead, I turned around, put my other hand on my hip, and glared at the four kids. "Bart is *not* my boyfriend," I hissed.

"Should I tell him that?" asked David Michael.

"Don't you dare!"

Karen was peeking out a window to make sure Bart was really the one who had rung the bell. (We are supposed to remember to do that so we don't fling open the door and find a stranger on our stoop.) "It *is* Bart . . . your boyfriend," she added devilishly.

"I know," I said.

"But you didn't check."

"But I was going to."

"Are you sure?"

"Nannie!" I yelled.

"What?" she replied.

"Your grandchildren are making me crazy!"

Nannie rescued me for the time being. She collected David Michael, Emily, Karen, and Andrew and took them upstairs to their playroom.

I was finally able to let poor Bart inside.

"Sorry about that," I told him. "Unfortunately, the kids are mildly bored today."

"No problem," said Bart, who is pretty easygoing.

Bart and I settled into the den with a large bowl of popcorn. I slipped *Uncle Buck* into the VCR. I turned around. Bart was sitting pretty much in the middle of the couch, the popcorn next to him.

Well, now what? Where was I supposed to sit?

Was the popcorn an invitation to join Bart on the couch? If I did that, I would have to sit *right next to him*. Would he think I was being too, oh, forward? I could sit in the armchair, but then I wouldn't be near the popcorn. Bart would have to stretch halfway across the room to pass it to me.

I solved the problem by sitting on the floor near Bart's feet, as if that was where I always sat to watch movies. Ten minutes later, Bart joined me on the floor. He sort of slid off the couch — very casually — until he was seated next to me. I reached back, found the popcorn bowl, and moved it to the floor, too. But I didn't reach for a handful until I saw Bart reach for one. Then I made sure our hands brushed against each other.

"Hee, hee, hee."

I distinctly heard a giggle.

Sure enough, Andrew was peeking into the room. Then he ducked out. A moment later, Emily pranced in. Her diaper was unfastened on one side and trailed down her leg. She waved gaily at Bart and me, then plopped onto the floor, blocking our view of the set. Oh, perfect, I thought.

Of course, by then I had snatched my hand out of the popcorn bowl. So had Bart. Andrew came back into the room, spotted the popcorn, and helped himself. He wiggled between Bart and me on the floor.

"What are you watching?" he asked. (He

sprayed Bart's face with popcorn as he·spoke.) "Can I watch, too?"

"You are," I muttered. Then I hoisted myself onto the couch. Bart followed me, wiping bits of corn kernels off his cheek.

I sat stiffly during the rest of *Uncle Buck* and the first half of *Back to the Future*. Karen joined us in the den. Andrew left, then returned with about thirty-five Matchbox cars. Nannie found Emily and put a new diaper on her — right there on the floor, in front of Bart.

My brothers and sisters talked endlessly to Bart, but I began to feel like the Tin Man in *The Wizard of Oz* — as if my jaw had rusted shut.

*Back to the Future* was nearly over when David Michael appeared in the doorway and announced, "Dinner's ready. Mom wants everyone to come to the table. That means you, Kristy. And your boyfriend."

I made a face at my brother.

Usually, my family eats meals at the big table in the kitchen. We had made an exception on Wednesday evening. In honor of Bart, Mom and Watson had set the table in the dining room. They had dimmed the lights and lit candles. I felt weirder than ever in that romantic setting with Bart to my left and Karen to my right, Watson jabbering about this an-

tique sale he'd been to, Emily humming the theme from *Sesame Street*, and Karen checking under the table every five minutes for some sign of her missing rat.

Since I am not noted for being quiet, Sam said, as Nannie and Charlie began to clear the table later, "What's the matter, Kristy? You aren't embarrassed, are you?"

And David Michael added, "Embarrassed about what? Her *boyfriend?*"

I glanced helplessly at my mother.

"David Michael," she said.

"Mom," he replied.

Emily knocked over her cup of milk.

I put my forehead in my hands.

And Karen jumped up, ran to a window, and exclaimed, "Hey, it's *really* snowing!"

# CHAPTER 7

## Jessi

Wednesday

I was prepared
for rehearsal. I had
been dancing my
legs off at home.
It wasn't that I
hadn't performed
in _The Nutcracker_
before. I had. But
I make a habit of
doing my absolute
best in any class,
rehearsal, or performance.
So on Wednesday
I was thinking about
Clara and Fritz and
their godfather
Drosselmeier, not
snow or icy roads

*Jessi*

or Quint. (Well, I
was thinking about
Quint a little bit.)

I was one of the BSC members who would
have had to miss the Wednesday meeting if
Kristy had decided to hold it. My ballet lessons
are very important to me. And so are the productions I dance in. I've performed parts in
*The Nutcracker* many times, but this was the
first year I was cast as the King of the Mice.
Usually, a boy plays that part, but I didn't
mind doing it — once.

The Wednesday rehearsal was crucial.
Opening night was less than a week away,
and every year *The Nutcracker* is the best-
attended ballet put on by my school. By my
ballet school, that is. The special dance school
I go to in Stamford. My teacher is Mme Noelle,
and she works her students *hard*. There's no
fooling around in Madame's classes.

That was how I managed to concentrate so
well on Wednesday. I *wanted* to think about
Quint. And under any other circumstances, I
would have done so, nonstop. I couldn't believe that in a few short hours I would be

seeing him again. And the visit would be a major one.

I guess I should back up a little. (I'm even confusing myself!) Quint and I met in New York when the members of the BSC were there for two wonderful weeks of summer vacation. Quint is a ballet dancer, too, and we met at the ballet. We had each gone to this special matinee performance of *Swan Lake* at Lincoln Center. We had gone alone — and we wound up sitting next to each other. Then we wound up talking. And finally we spent some time together. I met Quint's family, and I learned about Quint's dilemma. This was the thing. Quint is *such* a good dancer that his teacher thought he could be accepted at Juilliard, which is the performing arts school in New York City. Not just anyone can get into it. You have to audition and you have to be *good*. Quint didn't want to audition; not because he thought he wouldn't get in, but because he was afraid he *would* get in. See, the guys in Quint's neighborhood had been giving him a hard time about taking ballet lessons. (Quint used to sneak off to lessons with his shoes and things stuffed into a bowling ball bag.) Anyway, Quint and I talked a lot while I was in New York, and finally he decided just to *see* if he could get into Juilliard. So he auditioned, he did get in (naturally), and he decided to go. The guys still give him a hard time, but he just puts up with that. He doesn't even bother to use the bowling bag anymore.

I am extremely proud of Quint. And I miss him. I haven't seen him since we said good-bye in NYC. (Oh, by the way, Quint kissed me then. My first kiss. That is, my first meaningful kiss.) We've kept in touch, though, mostly by mail. We write to each other almost every day. Not necessarily a long letter, but a note or a postcard. Or sometimes I'll find a cartoon or an ad or anything funny, and I'll just drop it in an envelope and address it to Quint. We've spoken over the phone, too. That was how we'd made the arrangements for Quint to come to Stoneybrook for the first time.

And to be my date the night of the Winter Wonderland Dance.

While I was at the Wednesday rehearsal for *The Nutcracker*, Quint was on a train roaring toward Stamford. The train was supposed to get in just a few minutes before the end of my rehearsal. My dad was going to pick up first Quint and then me. After that, Quint was going to come back to Stoneybrook with us and stay until Saturday. We would go to the dance and still have time for a good long visit, and for Quint to get to know Mama and Daddy; my little sister, Becca; my baby brother, Squirt; and my Aunt Cecelia (Daddy's sister, who lives with us).

With the prospect of seeing Quint at the end of rehearsal, are you surprised I was able to concentrate at *all?* I was surprised. But Mme Noelle is very compelling. She really captures your attention. Even so, my mind wandered a few times, and I found myself hoping that my carefully laid plans would be carried out without any trouble. I hoped Quint's train would be on time. I hoped my rehearsal would end on time. I hoped Daddy wouldn't get delayed on his way into the city. Ordinarily, Daddy works in Stamford. (That was why we moved to Connecticut in the first place. The company Daddy works for transferred his job from New Jersey to Connecticut. Soon after we moved, I met my friends in the Baby-sitters Club.) On that Wednesday, however, Daddy had to go to a meeting in Stoneybrook! He planned to return to Stamford, though, after the meeting and pick up Quint and me.

"Doncers! Eyes to the front!" demanded Mme Noelle. She stood before us in the big rehearsal room at our school. Several assistant teachers were spread among the "doncers." (In case you couldn't tell, Mme Noelle is

French, and she speaks with an accent.)

The doncers straightened up. But a couple of the younger children were having some trouble concentrating for so long.

I nudged one of them, an eight-year-old girl named Sadie something. (I don't know the younger dancers all that well. They're not in my class, so I only see them at rehearsals or performances.) "Pay attention," I whispered to Sadie.

"But it's supposed to snow," she replied.

"Not a chance," I told her.

"The weatherman *said*."

Someone nudged me. "Jessi! Mme Noelle is staring at you." It was Katie Beth, a friend from my ballet class.

I braced myself for the sound of "Mademoiselle Romsey!" But it didn't come. The school secretary had tiptoed into the room and was whispering to one of the assistants, Mme Duprès. Mme Duprès frowned, nodded, signaled for Mme Noelle's attention, then whispered something to *her*.

Around me, Sadie and three other eight-year-olds (playing mice who fight alongside me, the Mouse King) sat on the floor, giggling.

"Come on, you guys. Stand up," I said. "The rehearsal isn't over."

"But my feet hurt," said Sadie.

"Mine, too," complained Danny.

"Mine, three," added Marcus and Wendy at the same time.

I couldn't blame them. The rehearsals had been growing longer and longer. The Wednesday rehearsal wasn't going to end until early evening. (So that no one would faint from starvation, the school kitchen had been stocked with crackers, packages of instant soup, and bags of dried fruit.)

Mme Noelle and Mme Duprès finished their conversation. Mme Duprès stepped back. I noticed that the secretary was still hovering in the doorway.

*"Mesdemoiselles et monsieurs,"* said Mme Noelle, clapping her hands for attention. (I guessed I was off the hook for having talked to Sadie during class.) "I have jost been eenformed zat eet eez snowing — "

"Yea!" shouted Sadie. She struck at the air with her fist and added, "Yes!" Then she realized that the rest of the class was silent — and staring at her. "Sorry," she said, and glanced helplessly at me.

"Apparently," Madame continued, "zee snow eez falling hard. Several of your parents have phoned to say zat zey are on zee way, or zat zey are *try*ing to be on zee way, but zat zey have been delayed."

"Huh?" said Danny.

"Who's delayed?" asked Wendy.

"Can I see the snow?" cried a six-year-old. Without waiting for an answer, she streaked out of the room and across the hallway to a window, stood on her tiptoes, and peered out. "Ooh, it *is* snowing!" she exclaimed. "I can't even see the street."

I glanced at the clock in the back of the room. We were supposed to rehearse for almost another hour. Even so, parents of some of the younger dancers would have arrived by this time, planning to watch the end of rehearsal.

But no parents were here yet.

Forty-five minutes later, still no parents arrived, although several more had called, saying that they were stuck somewhere, were held up, etc. One of the parents who had phoned was Daddy. His meeting was over, he said, but he was having trouble getting out of the parking lot. (Something to do with a stalled car.) He would be here as soon as he could.

At this point, Mme Noelle must have sensed that she was losing our attention, especially the attention of the younger kids. "All right. Rehearsal eez over," she announced. "You may change your clothes."

We scrambled for the changing rooms. (No

*Jessi*

parents showed up.) We changed our clothes. (No parents.) We stared outside at the whirling snow. (No parents.) Quint's train must have reached Stamford by now, I thought. And Daddy probably wasn't there to meet it. What was Quint doing?

I shivered. Suddenly I had a very bad feeling about the snow.

# CHAPTER 8

## Mary Anne

Wednesday

It finally snowed. No one could believe it. Even the weather forecasters seemed surprised. (Well, they'd been wrong for weeks. Predicting something that actually happened must have come as a shock to them.)

The snow didn't start until dinnertime, though, so it was a good thing the Pike kids had done their homework the night before. That morning, it was off to school as usual, for everyone except me.

What I mean is, it was off to school for me, too; it's just that it wasn't off as usual. "Off as usual" would have meant waking up in my own room and leaving from my own house. But on Wednesday, I left from the Pikes', having woken up jammed into the bedroom that Mallory and Vanessa share.

It was very early. I woke to the sounds of people trying to be quiet. There is nothing quite as disturbing as people who are *trying* to be quiet so they won't wake up other people, the ones who are sleeping. Mr. and Mrs. Pike were up long before the rest of us. They got up even before their alarm went off. Since Mal and her brothers and sisters and I didn't have to get up until after the Pikes had left, Mr. and Mrs. Pike were trying valiantly to let us sleep. Consequently, I could hear lots of whispers. Things like, "Shhh! Don't disturb the kids," and, "Turn down the radio. You're going to wake the whole neighborhood." Then I heard somebody tiptoe, tiptoe, tiptoe, and *crash!* into something he couldn't see because he hadn't turned on a light.

I never did go back to sleep. I lay on the cot and listened to the sounds of Mr. and Mrs. Pike making coffee, then warming up the car in the chilly garage, and finally leaving for the train station. I listened to Vanessa snoring lightly. I listened to Mal, who kept turning over and over in her bed. (She sleeps like an eggbeater.) Finally I heard the clock radio go off somewhere in the house. Then another one. Seconds later, a third went off practically in my ear.

*"There she was just a walkin' down the street, singin' do-wah-ditty-ditty-dum-ditty-do,"* blasted the radio.

"Oh," groaned Mal.

Vanessa woke up smiling. *"She looks good,"* she chimed in with the song. *"She looks fine. And I'm happy that she's mine."*

" 'Morning, Vanessa," I said. "Hey, Mal. Come on. Let's get going."

"Do-wah," said Mal.

Apparently, the Pikes had tuned all the radios in the house to the same oldies station. By the time I knocked on the door to the boys' room, a new song had come on. Nicky swung open the door and burst into the hallway, holding a hairbrush to his mouth, singing, *"Who put the bop in the bop-shoo-bop-shoo-bop?"* Seconds later, from the third bedroom, came the sound of Margo and Claire belting out, *"Who put the ram in the rama-lama-ding-dong?"*

By breakfast time, the eight kids and I were singing, *"Lollipop, lollipop, ooh-la-la-lolli-lolli-lollipop, lollipop, ooh-la-la . . ."*

"That's what I'd like for breakfast," said Margo, sliding into her place at the kitchen table. "A big orange lollipop. No, a purple one."

"Well, today's breakfast is toast and cereal and bananas. We don't have any lollipops. Sorry," I said.

"Bummer," replied Margo.

"Can I have a Popsicle?" asked Byron.

"A Popsicle?" I repeated. The Pike kids *are* allowed to eat pretty much whatever they want, but chocolate ice cream for breakfast? "I guess so," I said anyway. I looked at Mal, who shrugged.

"That's okay," said Byron. "I don't really want one. I just wanted to know if I could have one." He glanced out the window. "Some snow we got," he added.

"We're *never* going to get any snow," whined Vanessa.

"You say that every year," said Adam.

"Let's listen for a weather report," suggested Jordan.

When one came on a few minutes later, Mallory snorted. *"Heavy* snow?" she repeated. "Now they're saying *heavy* snow?"

"Maybe it will start this morning," said Nicky hopefully, "and school will close early and we'll get to leave before they assign homework."

"Maybe," I said, but when Mal and I left Claire, Margo, Nicky, Vanessa, and the triplets at Stoneybrook Elementary School, the sky was as relentlessly snow-free as ever, although the air *was* colder and damper than usual.

We said good-bye to the kids and Mal called, "Remember, Claire. Two sessions of kindergarten today. Stay with your teacher until we come for you in the afternoon." (Ordinarily, Claire goes to morning kindergarten, but that day she would stay for the second session as well, and then Mal and I would pick her up at the same time we picked up the other Pike kids.)

Nicky did not get his wish for an early closing of school. By the time the Pikes and I reached their house that afternoon, Mallory was actually laughing at the weather forecasters. "They said heavy snow developing quickly and starting before noon," she said, giggling. "Well, it's after three now."

"So the guy's a few hours late," said Jordan. "It could still snow."

"Yeah," agreed Byron, "especially if we do a snow dance."

"A what?" I asked.

"A snow dance. You know, like a rain dance. Only to make snow come."

"Let's do one now!" cried Vanessa.

"But you guys just took off your coats," said Mal.

"We'll put them back on," replied Adam.

A few minutes later, Mallory and I were standing in the backyard, watching her sisters and brothers stomp around, chanting, "Hey, come on, make it snow! Make it snow! Do-wah-ditty-ditty-dum-ditty-doe!"

At four o'clock, we called them inside. "Time to begin your homework," I said.

The triplets made faces. "I *know* we're not going to have school tomorrow," said Byron, but he didn't look as certain as he sounded.

Nevertheless, the boys began their homework, the radio playing in the background.

"Couldn't you think better with that off?" Mal asked them.

"We're listening for school closings," Jordan told her.

"But it *isn't snowing*," said Mal.

"*But it will be*," Nicky replied through clenched teeth.

Mallory sighed.

76

By six o'clock, we had finished our homework.

"Dinner!" Mal announced.

"What are you making?" asked Margo.

"Sloppy joes. You guys set the table while Mary Anne and I cook, okay?"

By the time we sat down to eat, the kids had finally given up on the snow. They sat glumly around the table, pushing their food back and forth across their plates.

Claire got up to pour herself another glass of milk. As she passed the window, she let out a yelp. "It's snowing!" she exclaimed.

"Very funny," mumbled Adam.

"No, really! It *is* snowing. Honest."

Every single person in the kitchen jumped up and joined Claire at the window. Sure enough, tiny flakes were falling. They were kind of hard to see, though.

"We'll probably get two inches," I said.

"Do they close school for two inches?" asked Nicky.

"No, dork," Jordan said witheringly to his brother. "Anyway, I bet it's just a flurry."

The snow was still falling when we began to clear the table.

"You know, it's starting to fall harder," I said to Mal.

"It's sticking," she added.

"Can we play in it?" asked Nicky. "Before it melts?"

"Why not?" replied Mal. "Your homework is done."

Once again, the kids dressed to go outdoors. Only now they added boots and snowpants to their outfits. I turned on the light in the backyard. "Stay away from the road, you guys," I called as the Pikes hurtled outside.

The snow was not only sticking, it was beginning to pile up. And it was falling thickly. I couldn't see very far in front of me. "Do you suppose the weatherman was finally right?" I asked Mal.

"I guess he had to be sometime," she replied.

"Yum, tasty snow!" exclaimed Claire. She was walking around with her tongue sticking out, catching flakes on it. "Mm. Mint-flavored."

Vanessa stuck out her tongue, too. "Mine's cherry. Very cherry."

"You girls are crazy," pronounced Nicky. Then he shouted "Crumble!" to Claire, who obeyed.

*Pow!* A snowball exploded against Nicky's back.

"No snowball fights!" yelled Mallory.

"Darn," replied Adam. Then he turned to

his littlest sister. "Hey, Claire, did you know that if we get enough snow, the Abominable Snowman appears?"

"He does?" answered Claire.

"Yup. He rises out of the snow in the yard. Then he comes in the house and turns children under six into Popsicles."

"Oh, yeah?" replied Claire. "How can he come inside? He'd melt."

"Not the *Abom*inable Snowman. He's magic," Adam told her.

"You mean like Frosty?"

"Yes. Only Frosty is nice and the Abominable Snowman is . . . a monster."

"Yikes!" shrieked Claire.

"Okay, okay. I think it's time to go in," I said. The snow wasn't showing any signs of stopping; besides, I didn't want the Abominable Snowman story to get out of hand. "Come on, everybody."

Inside, Mal and I helped the younger kids take off their wet clothes. We draped damp mittens and hats around the laundry room. Then we threw wet socks in the dryer. After that, Mal made hot chocolate and we sat around the kitchen table, steaming mugs in front of us.

"You know, school might be closed tomorrow, after all," I said.

"We did our homework for nothing then," said Nicky, pouting.

"For nothing?! Hey, you'll have a free day tomorrow," Mal told her brother.

"Well, *I* didn't have any homework anyway," said Claire smugly.

"That's good," replied Adam, "because the Abominable Snowman also steals homework."

## Dawn

Wednesday Evening

The ride to the airport was totally scary. Even though I can't drive, and even though I was sitting in the front seat, I turned into an awful backseat driver. I thought Mom was going to throw me out of the car. "Dawn!" she kept saying. "Relax!" Which isn't very relaxing when someone is screeching the words in your ear, and at the same time gripping the steering wheel so tightly her knuckles had probably turned white (she was wearing gloves, so I couldn't tell for sure), and then leaning forward so her nose was an eighth of an inch from the windshield...

## Dawn

When I arrived home from school on Wednesday, I found my mom in a nervous state, which is not comforting to a thirteen-year-old. I knew something was wrong when I walked through the door and came upon Mom dusting the living room. The fact that she was at home during the day wasn't what was weird. Mom works, but she'd told me earlier that she had arranged to take this day off. The weird thing was that she was dusting. My mom is *not* a cleaner. Or a washer or a cooker or a sewer (that's as in "person who sews," not as in "smelly underground tunnel"). She can *do* those things all right, but she would prefer not to. Mary Anne's dad is the organized, domestic adult in the family. Mom is a scatterbrain who would rather do just about anything besides pick up a dust rag.

"What's wrong?" I asked Mom, closing the front door behind me.

Mom looked up. I don't think she'd heard the door open.

"Hi, sweetie," she said. "I don't know. I don't like the sound of the weather report."

"What's the report?"

"For heavy snow."

"Oh, Mom. They've been saying that for

days now. Have you seen one flake of snow? Have you even seen a drop of *rain?*"

"No," she admitted.

"Besides, what's so bad about snow?" I meant, what's so bad about it apart from the fact that it's freezing cold and wet? As a California girl, I am rarely warm enough in Connecticut. Oh, sure, California isn't the tropics. It has its share of cold, damp weather. But nothing like Connecticut's freezing winters. And I had certainly never seen snow where I lived in California. Winter in the East had been sort of a shock.

However, my mother had grown up in Stoneybrook. "You used to drive in snow all the time, Mom," I pointed out.

"Yes, but I didn't like it. California was a huge relief."

"Well, think about Jeff instead."

"I have been. This is not good flying weather."

"He doesn't get airsick."

"He gets scared, though."

I sighed. Every now and then I feel as if I am my mother's mother. "In a few hours he'll be here, your worrying will be over, and we'll start a wonderful winter vacation," I said. "Personally, I am excited."

Finally Mom smiled. "I am, too. And bored. I'm finished with the dusting." (She had dusted, like, one end table and a couple of chair legs.)

Guess what. By the time we left for the airport, it was *snowing*. I could not believe it. The weather forecaster had finally been right. (Well, I suppose in Connecticut, if you constantly predict snow, you're bound to be right occasionally.)

Mom was a wreck.

"Why don't I ride to the airport with you?" Richard asked Mom. (Richard is Mary Anne's father.)

"Oh, honey, that's okay," said Mom. (If Mary Anne had been home, she and I would have exchanged a smile. We always do when we hear our parents call each other "honey" or "sweetheart" or something. Jeff just says, "Gross me out.") "I'm sure we'll be fine. I should get used to snow again. Besides, you promised Mary Anne you'd be home in case she or Mallory needs you."

"Are you sure?" asked Richard.

"Positive." Mom smiled. (Sort of.)

So we took off. Mom had insisted on leaving *way* before Jeff's plane was due in. As it turned out, that was smart. Mom backed down the driveway at a crawl, then edged onto the road. Okay, so it was snowing a little. About an inch had collected on the ground. But I didn't see what the big deal was. Surely she could speed up to, oh, ten miles an hour.

No way. It turned out Mom knew what she was doing. As she crept toward the stop sign at the end of our street (which took about twenty minutes) I felt her put on the brakes — very gently. And the next thing I knew, our car was slipping eerily to the right, to the left, and to the right again. I looked around frantically, trying to see what we might crash into — the stop sign, a mailbox, a phone pole. Is this it? I wondered. Is this how I'm going to die? By sliding, on an inch of snow at five miles an hour, into the Bahadurians' mailbox? (Which, by the way is shaped like a cow.)

Well, we did run into the cow mailbox, but since we were moving so slowly, we barely bumped it. In fact, we touched it just hard enough so that some of the snow that had landed on the cow's head showered to the ground.

Nevertheless, I heard Mom say a word I have never heard her use before. In fact, I've heard it only in movies that Mom doesn't know I've seen.

"Mom!" I gasped. I was more stunned by what she had said than by the fact that we'd had an accident while our house was still in view.

"Sorry, honey," she murmured. She straightened out the car, and soon we were on our way again, Mom all tight-lipped and gripping the steering wheel. Once we reached a main road, the driving wasn't quite so horrible. As the snow fell, it was turned to slush by the wheels of the cars that ground over it. The slush wasn't as slippery as the unplowed snow. Plus, the road wasn't as dark. It was lit by street lamps.

"The highway will be a piece of cake," I said to Mom.

Wrong. The snow was falling more thickly by the time Mom inched onto the highway. And there weren't as many cars on the highway as there had been in downtown Stoneybrook. The few cars that did come by were edging along like Mom. This was when I turned into the backseat driver.

"It's getting windy," I murmured, flakes swirling before our headlights. "Go slowly, Mom."

"Right."

"And the snow is sticking. No slush."

Grimly, Mom drove on.

"We could turn around," I said in a small voice.

"Go back?" replied Mom. She shook her head. "Jeff would be stranded at the airport. Then he'd *really* feel abandoned."

"Oh, yeah."

We continued in silence. Finally, I glanced at my watch. "Hey, we're late!" I exclaimed. "At least, we're going to be late."

Mom shook her head. "All we can do is keep moving. Jeff will wait for us. He'll probably call Richard."

"And Richard will tell him how long ago we left the house and then Jeff will think we've been in an accident."

"Dawn, I — "

"Mom, look out!" I screamed.

On the other side of the highway, on the other side of the *median strip*, the headlights of a Mack truck wavered as its wheels skidded. Then the truck bumped off the highway, heading for the snow-covered divider — and for our car.

I covered my eyes with my hands and prayed that my seat belt would do whatever it was supposed to do. A second later I felt our car swerve.

Then Mom said that word again.

I dared to open my eyes.

Somehow, the truck was back where it belonged. It was still across the median strip. It had run into the car in front of it (and we had nearly run into a van in the right lane), but I didn't think anyone was hurt. I could see the drivers of the truck and the car opening their doors and climbing out to examine the damage.

"A fender bender," said Mom through clenched teeth.

"Oh, my lord," I muttered. "I thought we were dead." I started to shake and couldn't stop, even though Mom turned up the heat.

During the rest of the torturous drive I could do nothing but look at the cars around us and yelp for Mom to be careful. Also, I kept announcing how late we were. "Jeff's plane landed ten minutes ago." . . . "Jeff's plane landed fifteen minutes ago."

"Dawn, I am doing my best," said Mom. "Would you relax?"

"Jeff is going to be in a panic!" I cried.

No answer.

Somehow, we reached the airport. Mom found a parking spot near the entrance. (The lot was mostly empty.) Then we hurried inside. Mom had phoned the airport before we left, so she knew the gate where Jeff's plane had landed.

I grabbed her hand. "Come on!" I said, and we raced through the airport.

# CHAPTER 10

## Stacey

Wednesday Evening

My hair looked great. It really did. Joyce had performed a miracle. (Mom gave her a big tip.) I was so enthralled with it that I looked at myself in every mirror between the salon and the exit to the parking lot. I barely even thought about the snow. A few minutes later, everything was switched around. My hair was forgotten and I could think of nothing but the snow. And my mom. It is not fun to be a kid watching your mother become frightened.

To be honest, I'm not sure whether Mom tipped Joyce so well because of the good work she'd done or because Mom was distracted by the woman who had come into the salon and announced that it was snowing. It could have been the snow since, as I mentioned, my mother is not very experienced at driving in it. At any rate, Joyce looked awfully pleased with her tip.

Mom rushed me out of the salon before I'd even put on my coat.

"Hurry up, sweetie," she said.

"Let me get my coat on."

"You can do that while we're walking."

Walking? Ha. Mom dragged me through the mall at sixty miles an hour. We were moving so fast that I hadn't, in fact, managed to shrug into my jacket by the time we reached the exit.

Mom frowned as she waited for me to zip up.

"What?" I exclaimed, exasperated. "You want me to go out in that with no jacket?" Then I just *had* to cover my head so my wonderful new perm wouldn't get wet.

I thought Mom would have a cow.

But I forgot about my hair, my jacket, everything, the second Mom opened the door. When she did so, a gust of snow blasted us. That is how fast the snow was moving: It actually hurt our faces.

I thought Mom would close the door and come right back inside. But no, she set her jaw and continued toward the car. I hustled behind her, shielding my eyes from the stinging snowflakes.

We found the car, which was a wonder. The lot was full of snow-covered lumps. How Mom could tell our snow-covered lump from all the others is beyond me, but she could. She aimed right for it. She must be equipped with special Mother Radar.

In a flash she had unlocked the doors, and we were sitting in the car with the defroster and the windshield wipers going. The wipers were not strong enough to clear the windows, though. Mom had to get out and work on them from the outside with an ice scraper. Then she slid into the driver's seat again.

She turned to look at me. "Ready?" she asked.

"I guess so." I removed the scarf from my head and shook out my hair.

"Phew!" exclaimed Mom as she turned the key in the ignition. "Your hair — "

"I know. My hair smells like rotten eggs."

"Well . . . yes."

I giggled. "I thought moms were supposed to be supportive."

"Oh, we are, we are." My mother started the car, and we pulled out of our parking place and inched through the lot to the exit.

"You okay?" I asked Mom. She was hunched over the steering wheel, leaning forward to peer through the windshield.

Mom nodded. "It's hard to see, that's all."

We reached the end of the ramp leading to the highway, and Mom looked over her shoulder. She looked for so long that I finally said, "Ahem."

"I still can't see very well, Stace. The snow is awfully thick."

"Oh. I don't mind if we go slowly."

Mom eased onto the highway. "Not bad!" she exclaimed a few moments later. "The highway is clearer than the other roads were. I think we'll make it."

"Yes. We are survivors," I said seriously. "Intrepid snow explorers. We should be written up for 'Drama in Real Life,' and our story should appear in *Reader's Digest*. Don't you think?"

Mom smiled. "Let's see. The title would read, um . . . 'BLIZZARD!' "

"Yeah," I agreed. " 'BLIZZARD!' And the

story would tell how these two gorgeous young women — "

"Thank you, thank you," interrupted Mom.

" — who have just spent a grueling afternoon malling and getting their hair permed, climb into the family car — "

I stopped short.

Which is exactly what the car in front of us had done. With no warning, it just stopped. I mean, its brake lights flashed on, but only a split second before the car stopped moving. Instinctively, Mom slammed on her brakes.

We fishtailed across the highway.

I screamed. (I couldn't help it.)

"Stacey, be *quiet!*" said Mom, but I don't think she was aware that she'd spoken.

I was sure we were going to slide right into another car, or that another car was going to slide into us.

But that didn't happen. We came to a stop in the left lane. I rubbed away the frost on my window and tried to see why the driver of the other car had slammed on his brakes. But I couldn't make out anything through the snow.

"That does it," said my mother.

"What do you mean?"

"We are getting off the highway. We'll take the back roads home."

"Why?"

"Because there are too many cars on the highway. Too many crazy drivers. There are probably accidents everywhere. I don't want us to find ourselves in the middle of a pileup." Mom began to guide the car across the highway, back to the right lane. "We'll get off at the next exit," she said.

"Are you sure you know the way from here?" I asked.

"Yup," replied Mom. "Stop worrying, honey. I'll get us home safely."

We passed two fender benders before we reached the exit. "See?" Mom said. "We don't want to end up in one of those situations."

"Boy, I'm sure glad Claudia didn't come with us. We'd never have been back in time for her to sit at the Perkinses' house tonight."

My mom almost drove by the next exit ramp. Not that it would have made much difference, since she was going so slowly. At any rate, she did turn onto it and soon we were traveling through the countryside. (At least, I think that's what we were traveling through. I couldn't see anything except snow.)

"I guess the weatherman was right after all," Mom commented.

"What? Oh, yeah. I guess he was. . . . Mom, are you *positive* you know how to get home from here? I mean, are you absolutely positive?''

Mom gave me a Look. "We're not lost," she said.

"Well, do you know where we are?"

"Honey, if I didn't know where we *were* then I wouldn't know where to *go*. Relax, okay? Don't you have something to do?"

"You mean, did I remember to bring along a coloring book and crayons?"

Mom laughed. "Sorry. I'm a little nervous. Put on a tape or turn on the radio, okay?"

"No problem." I turned on the radio, and tuned it to this rock station I love. Two songs belted out before I said, "Don't you want the classical station, Mom?" She was concentrating so hard on driving that she didn't hear me.

After several more minutes passed she said, "This snow is really *thick*. It's sticking, too. There are already several inches on the road."

I didn't know whether to feel glad because undoubtedly this meant . . . NO SCHOOL the next day! Or to feel worried because there we were, on some dark back road in the middle of nowhere, being practically buried by snow.

"Do you think this is a blizzard?" I asked.

Mom shook her head. (I think she meant to say, "I don't know.")

I stared outside, gazing at the storm. I remembered snowstorms in New York. I remembered watching the flakes whirl by my bedroom window. Sometimes the wind swept them *up* in a funnel.

"It's really coming down," my mother would say then.

"It's really going up," my father would say.

I was thinking about city blizzards when I realized that Mom had stopped the car.

"What's wrong? What are you doing?" I asked. (For some reason, I was panicky immediately. *My* radar was picking up signals. My Kid Radar.)

"I think I better wait until the snow has let up a bit," Mom replied. "It's just too thick right now. I can't see more than a couple of feet in front of me." She had stopped by the side of the road.

One thing I did not worry about was being hit by some unsuspecting car from behind. This was because, for one thing, we hadn't seen a single car or truck or even a pedestrian since we had left the highway. For another thing, Mom left our headlights on so that we *could* be seen. She also left on the heater. We would have turned to icicles without it.

Mom and I chatted and pretended we weren't nervous in the least about what was happening. I kept checking my watch and saying things like, "In ten minutes we should be on our way again."

When a half hour had passed, Mom resolutely turned on the ignition again. "The snow isn't any lighter," she said. "Well, all right. I'll just drive again. We'll reconcile ourselves to a long trip home, that's all."

Mom put her foot on the accelerator. She pressed down. She pressed harder.

I could feel our back wheels spinning.

Mom groaned. Then, as if she were moving in slow motion, she leaned forward until her head was resting on the steering wheel. "This isn't happening," she muttered.

My stomach turned to a block of ice. "Now what?" I asked.

Mom gathered herself together. "I'll try to move the car," she replied. Which was sort of ridiculous because she wouldn't let me work the accelerator while she pushed the car, and she also wouldn't let me go out and push.

"I don't want you to get hurt," she said.

Mom rocked the car a few times, then rushed around and tried to drive us out of the snowy rut our wheels had created. It was no use.

We were stuck.

We were stranded.

## Kristy

Wednesday Evening

I thought the afternoon with Bart and my family had been excruciating. That was just because the evening hadn't happened yet. Oh, I know my disastrous adventure was nothing compared to, say, Stacey's, but it was a disaster on a different level.... Well, it was.

Okay, it sort of was.

"Liar!" cried David Michael.

Karen was still standing at the window. "I am not a liar," she said indignantly. "It really is snowing. Come look."

"Ha. I'm not falling for that," said my brother. "That's like telling someone his shoe is untied when he's wearing loafers."

Karen paused. Then she hissed, "David Michael, XYZ. Your fly is open."

David Michael grew beet red. He looked down, then up. "No, it isn't!" he exclaimed.

"Gotcha!" cried Karen. "Now come and look at the snow. I'm not kidding about it. I bet school will be closed tomorrow."

I put my head in my hands. Why did Karen have to go and mention *flies* in front of Bart? To make things worse, Bart leaned over to me and whispered, "What does XYZ mean?"

Karen heard him.

"It means 'examine your zipper'!" she called from across the room. "Get it? X-amine Your Zipper? XYZ?"

Oh, please. Somebody put me out of my misery.

David Michael did, although he wasn't aware of it. He shouted, "Hey, Karen's telling the truth! It *is* snowing!"

100

Which caused a stampede to the dining room windows. Even I looked.

"A real storm," said Charlie admiringly.

"I'm going to turn on the radio," announced Sam. And he did. He tuned the little kitchen radio to WSTO while we cleared the dining room table. As we carried plates and dishes back and forth, we heard one of the weather forecasters say, "Well, folks, the storm *has* hit. Better late than never! You can expect a foot or more of snow before this blows over!" He sounded jubilant. I guess he was pleased with his prediction.

"A foot or more!" repeated David Michael, awestruck.

"I wouldn't count on it," said Watson. He flicked off the radio. "We rarely get snows like that. We're too close to the ocean."

"Oh, bullfrogs," said Karen.

"Maybe I should go home now," Bart spoke up.

"Why don't you wait awhile?" Watson replied. "Until it lets up a little. I don't really want to drive in that."

"Oh, I can walk," Bart assured him. (The Taylors live close by.)

"Oh, no," said Mom. "In the dark? In the wind?" (You'd think we lived in Alaska or someplace.)

"I'm tough," kidded Bart.

"Seriously, just wait a half hour or so," said Watson. "Then I'll drive you."

"Is that all right with your parents?" asked Mom. "Can you stay a little longer? When are they expecting you home?"

"Not for awhile," said Bart cheerfully.

"Great. Let's have dessert, then." Sam had opened the door to the refrigerator. He pretty much lives in the fridge. He knows its contents by heart. "I hope that pie is still in the freezer," he said, and opened the freezer compartment to check. Sure enough, there was the pie. Store-bought, frozen, blueberry. "Won't this be excellent with vanilla ice cream?" Sam went on. (Of course, there was ice cream, too. It was behind the pie, where no one could see it, but Sam sensed its presence.)

Nannie stuck the pie in the microwave while Charlie and I set out plates, spoons, forks, and recycled paper napkins. Bart and my family and I ate warm blueberry pie à la mode in the kitchen. It was all very casual. Emily sat in her high chair, Sam and David Michael sat on the counters, Karen (for some reason) sat on the floor, and everyone else sat at the table.

I watched Karen eat her dessert. First she knocked the ice cream off the pie. Then she ate the pie filling. Then she ate the crust. Then she stirred the ice cream into vanilla soup. Then she drank her "soup" from the plate. Finally she ran into the bathroom, where apparently she checked herself in the mirror, because she charged right back out, crying, "Look at me! I'm sick! I have a blue tongue. And blue teeth. I have the winter blues."

Bart burst out laughing. "That's a good joke!"

I whispered to him, "I'm not sure she knows what she said."

"Well, it's still funny."

We finished our desserts and piled the dishes in the sink. Karen began to prance around the kitchen, singing, *"Oh, the weather outside is frightful. But the fire inside's delightful. Da, da, da, da, da, doe, doe, doe. Let it snow, let it snow, let it snow!* . . . Thank you! Thank you, ladies and gentlemen."

"Oh, wonderful," I said to Mom. "What a good idea. Pie à la mode. We should be sure to give Karen a big load of sugar every night right before her bedtime. Especially when we have a guest."

Mom smiled at me. "Honey, Bart has a little brother. I'm sure he's used to the things kids do. Just relax."

"Is he used to that?" I pointed to Karen, who was wearing her sweater-pants again. She was modeling them for Bart as she sang, *"In the meadow we will build a snowman, and pretend that he is Parson Brown . . ."*

"Well, Karen gets excited about things," said Mom. "You remember how thrilling snow was when you were seven, don't you?"

"Sure," I replied. "I just hope I never danced around in sweater-pants, singing old songs in front of someone's important boyfriend."

Why, I wondered, had I wanted Bart to have a chance to get to know my family? They were embarrassing me beyond all reason.

Later, Bart and my brothers and Karen and I were watching TV. Watson was putting Emily Michelle to bed. Mom and Nannie were talking in the living room. "Kristy?" said Bart.

"Yeah?"

"I should probably go home now. It's getting kind of late."

"Okay." I looked out the window. "Gosh, it's snowing as hard as ever. I wonder if Watson will want to drive yet. Come on. We'll talk to Mom." Bart and I went into the living room. "Mom? Bart says he should be getting home, but it's still snowing really hard," I told her.

"I can walk," Bart offered again.

"I don't know," said Mom.

"I'm going to check outside," I announced. I opened the front door. Then I tried to push open the storm door. "Hey, it's stuck," I exclaimed. I pushed harder.

Watson appeared behind me and flicked on the porch light.

"Wow!" I cried. "Look at that! No wonder I couldn't open the door." Snow was piled against it, blown there by the wind. "Hey, this is a real storm," I added. "Not just some snow shower. . . . How is Bart going to get home? He can't go out in a storm." (I knew Watson wasn't about to haul out his car, even if he *had* just put on its snow tires.)

"Bart, why don't you spend the night here?" suggested Mom.

Spend the night. What a ridiculously simple solution to the problem. Why hadn't I thought of it? No. Wait. *Bart* spend the night at *my* house with *my* family? Was I on a suicide mission?

"Um, Mom," I said hoarsely, "I don't think that's a very good idea."

Unfortunately, Bart answered my mother at the same time. "Oh, thanks, Mrs. Brewer. That would be wonderful. I'll call my parents."

I was torn. I didn't know whether to follow Bart to the kitchen or stay behind to question the sanity of my mother. Finally, I just mouthed "ARE YOU CRAZY?" to Mom, then followed Bart.

In the kitchen, Bart picked up the phone, dialed his number, and spoke to his dad. "Yeah, dinner was great. . . . Mm-hmm. . . . Blueberry pie. . . . So, anyway, Kristy's mother said I might as well just spend the night. Is that okay? I'll see you — I'll see you — Dad? Dad?" Bart turned to me. "The line went dead," he reported.

The words had barely left his mouth when everything went dark. I could hear appliances turning off throughout the house. The TV flicked off, a radio flicked off, even the refrigerator turned itself off.

"Uh-oh. Power failure," I said needlessly.

From the TV room, Andrew shrieked. "Turn on the lights!" he cried.

"Andrew hates the dark," I informed Bart. I found a flashlight, and we made our way into the den. "The storm must have knocked down the power lines," I said to Andrew. "It'll be okay."

Andrew was hugging my legs and sniffling. Karen looked worried. "I hope the lights come on before Christmas," she said.

And Bart said, "I'm glad I was able to talk to my dad."

Mom and Nannie and Watson joined us in the den with some more flashlights. "We might as well go to bed now," said Watson.

David Michael snorted. "Where's Bart going to sleep? In Kristy's room?"

"No, Toast-for-Brains," I said. "We'll give him a guest room."

Going to bed had never been more excruciating. I couldn't, of course, let Bart see me in my pajamas. This meant I had to wait until everybody was finished using the bathroom. Then I went in, quickly washed my face and brushed my teeth, and darted back to my room. I locked the door behind me before I changed out of my clothes. We are not supposed to sleep with our doors locked (in case of fire), but I didn't want Bart accidentally sleepwalking into my room during the night or something. I lay awake until almost one o'clock, trying to figure out what to do, and also wondering what my friends had been up to that evening. At 12:53 I finally dared to unlock the door. Then I leapt into bed and huddled under the covers, very aware of the fact that Bart was sleeping just a couple of rooms down the hall.

How was a person supposed to relax under

such conditions? And, oh lord, what would happen the next morning when I woke up, bleary-eyed and fuzzy-tongued? I could not let Bart see me that way.

I set my alarm for five-thirty.

# CHAPTER 12

## Claudia

Wednesday Evening

I always have fun when I sit for Mariah and Gabie and Laura. They are such good kids. Just like evry other kid in stoneybrook they were realy exited for the snow. As soon as the flacks started to fall, maria began to plan how to spend Thrusday. "I no I wont have school" she said. "We can go sleding and billed snow peopul and maybe make hot choclate." She and gabie were so so happy. Of course that was befor the lights went out and the phone stoped working.

My job at the Perkinses' started at six o'clock on Wednesday evening, as soon as I had finished taking the BSC calls. On my way across the street, I realized it was snowing — just tiny little flakes, but they were better than nothing.

The house the Perkins girls live in, the one across the street from me, is pretty special. Guess why. It used to be Kristy's house. She and her mother and Sam and Charlie and David Michael lived there before Kristy's mom married Watson and the Thomases moved to his mansion. Myriah Perkins, who's five and a half, sleeps in Kristy's old room now. She has two younger sisters — Gabbie, who's almost three, and Laura, who's a baby. My friends and I love to sit for the Perkinses.

I knew that the girls (well, the older two) would be glad to hear about the snow, so as soon as Myriah and Gabbie opened the door, I said, "Surprise! It's snowing!"

"All *right!*" Gabbie exclaimed, and bounced onto the porch in her sock feet.

"Whoa," I said. "You'll freeze with no shoes on. Come inside with me."

"Mommy and Daddy are going to dinner at the Vansants'," Myriah said as I ushered Gabbie inside. "The Vansants live way, way out in the country. They live on a farm. They have a *horse!*"

"Cool," I said.

"Hello, Claudia," Mrs. Perkins greeted me. She placed Laura in her bouncy chair. (The chair is suspended from the top of a door frame. It's mounted on springs. Laura bounces happily in it every day now.)

"Hi," I replied. "Hi, Mr. Perkins. Hi, Laura. Guess what. It's starting to snow."

"You're kidding," said Mr. Perkins. "Huh. The weatherman was right."

"We'll have to be extra careful on the roads," said Mrs. Perkins to her husband.

"Oh, it's just a dusting," I went on. "No big deal."

The Perkinses gave me instructions for the evening — what to fix for dinner, when to put the girls to bed, where to find the Vansants' phone number. "We'll be home before ten," added Mr. Perkins.

"Okay, you guys. Who's hungry?" I said when Mr. and Mrs. Perkins had left.

"Me!" said Myriah.

"I want Mommy," said Gabbie.

"She'll be here when you wake up tomorrow," I assured her. "And I'll tell her to kiss you good night when she comes home. Is that okay?"

Gabbie nodded.

"I would like her to kiss me, too," said Myriah politely.

"Okay. Now — I am going to fix supper. Laura can bounce in her chair. Myriah, why don't you and Gabbie keep a watch on the snow for me? You can give me a weather report at dinner. The living room window can be Weather Central, like on the news."

"Yeah!" exclaimed Myriah. "Gabbie, come on. We have an important job to do."

Mrs. Perkins had told me that a pot of leftover spaghetti was in the fridge. I heated that up in the double boiler while I threw together a salad. Then I set out Laura's baby food.

"Dinner!" I called.

Myriah and Gabbie came running. As I lifted Laura out of her bouncy seat and placed her in her high chair, Myriah announced, "We have a weather report for you. Outside, it is very, very cold. We think the wind is starting to blow. And the snowflakes are bigger now."

"There's snow all over the grass," added Gabbie. "Everywhere."

Maybe I should have paid more attention to the girls' report. But I didn't. I was too busy serving spaghetti, feeding Laura, and trying to feed myself. Then, in the middle of all *that*,

Myriah said, "I think the pets are hungry."

"The pets!" I cried. I had forgotten to feed them. Mrs. Perkins had said to put their food out while we were eating dinner.

The pets are Chewbacca, a wonderful, lovable, but slightly crazy black Labrador retriever; a cat, R.C., which stands for Rat-Catcher; and a new kitten, Socks Sebastian Perkins, known as Socks. (His fur is orange everywhere except on his feet, which are white, so he looks as if he's wearing two pairs of socks.)

I filled Chewbacca's dish with yucky dog food, and the cats' dishes with Kibbles. Then I gave them fresh water.

"Okay, Laura. Now you can eat," I said, aiming a spoonful of mashed carrots toward her mouth.

Laura opened her mouth obediently. She took the carrot goo — but she didn't swallow it. She smiled, then laughed, and the next thing I knew, I was wearing carrots across my front. Luckily, I had prepared myself for this possibility. I've fed enough babies to know that they shouldn't be the only ones wearing bibs.

"I am so, so happy it is snowing," said Myriah from the end of the table. "I don't think

I will have to go to kindergarten tomorrow."

"Don't you like kindergarten?" Gabbie asked her sister.

"Yes," replied Myriah. "I do. It's fun. But tomorrow the snow will be even funner. We can go sledding in the backyard."

"And make a snowman!" added Gabbie.

"Or a whole snow family!" cried Myriah. "A snow mommy and a snow daddy and three snow girls and a snow dog and two snow cats."

"You are going to be very busy tomorrow," I said.

"That's what happens when you're five," Myriah replied.

Myriah and Gabbie finished their supper and ate apples for dessert. Laura scarfed up her carrots and some beef baby food and drank some milk.

"Guys?" I said to Myriah and Gabbie. "I'm going to put Laura to bed in a few minutes. Can you play upstairs until I'm finished? Then I'll come downstairs with you."

I carried Laura up to her room. I was followed by Myriah and Gabbie, who detoured into Gabbie's room to look at picture books.

"Okay, Laura-Lou," I said. I laid her in her crib and took off her blue overalls. I changed her diaper. Then I slipped her into a fuzzy yellow sleeper. Finally, I switched on her music box and night-light, and turned off the lamp on her dresser. "Sleep tight," I said, rubbing her back. I tiptoed out of the room.

From down the hall I could hear Myriah chanting, "Run, run as fast as you can." And Gabbie chiming in with, "You can't catch me, I'm the Gingerbread Man!"

The girls kept me busy that evening. They had invented a game they wanted me to play with them. They decided they needed milk and cookies. They wanted to watch a TV show, which I couldn't seem to find, no matter how many times I flipped through the stations. They played a noisy game of tag with Socks, who kept running into small places where he couldn't be reached.

Finally, I had to announce, "Bedtime." I knew this would not be greeted with cheers or squeals of delight. However, I was somewhat surprised when, instead of "Do we *have* to, Claudia?" I heard *ring, ring!*

"Telephone!" cried Gabbie. "Can I get it?"

"I think I better," I answered. "But you can say hello." I picked up the receiver. "Hello, Perkins residence. This is Claudia."

"Hi, Claudia. It's Mr. Perkins."

"Oh! Hi. Is everything all right?"

"Technically, yes. But . . . Mrs. Perkins and

I aren't going to be able to come home tonight. The roads are *awful*. They're slippery, and most of them aren't plowed. We left early, but we had to turn around and come back."

"Wow," I exclaimed. "I didn't think the snow was that bad."

"Neither did we, until we tried to drive in it. We're at the Vansants' house now, and we're going to spend the night here. Do you think you could stay with the girls? I know it's asking a lot. Or maybe you could take them over to your house. Are your parents home?"

"Yup. Don't worry about anything. I'll work this out. The girls will be fine."

I let both Gabbie and Myriah talk to their parents for a few moments. When they'd finished, I called my own parents and told them what had happened.

"I'll be right over," said my mother.

"Oh, you don't have to come. Honest. It's awful outside. We'll be all right. And if anything does happen I can just call you or come over. Okay?"

"Okay," agreed Mom.

We hung up. I could hardly contain my excitement. What an adventure this was! Baby-sitting by myself, overnight, for three kids, including a baby. I would have some story to tell my BSC friends. Suddenly, I felt like calling them. We could talk for a few minutes and catch up with each other. I wanted to find out how Stacey's perm looked, whether Dawn was back from the airport . . .

"Claudia?" said a little voice. It was Gabbie. I stopped daydreaming and looked down at her. "Mommy isn't going to kiss me good night tonight. You said she would, but she isn't coming home."

"Oh, Gabbers. I'm sorry," I replied. "I didn't realize we were having a big snowstorm. But you know what? Your mommy and daddy will be home tomorrow" (I hoped) "and they can both kiss you then. So I think you guys should say good night to Socks and R.C. and Chewy now. It's almost bedtime."

"Okay," agreed Gabbie, looking tearful but brave.

Myriah and Gabbie found the cats. They said good night to them, and kissed their tails. Then they went off in search of Chewbacca.

You'd think a large, noisy dog would be easy to find. But the girls looked in Chewy's favorite spots and didn't see any sign of him.

"I bet he's in the laundry room," said Myriah.

No Chewy.

"Maybe he's under the big table," said Gabbie. "He takes naps there."

117

We looked under the dining room table. No Chewy.

"Okay, we'll search the house," I announced.

The girls and I looked through every room. We looked in tiny places where Chewbacca couldn't possibly fit. Gabbie even looked in Laura's crib. No Chewy. We called and whistled and whistled and called.

"Chewy is missing!" Myriah announced tearfully.

"Calm down," I said to the girls. "I'll call Mom and Dad. They'll know what to do. They can come over and help us."

I reached for the phone, started to dial our number, and realized the phone was dead. No dial tone. "Uh-oh," I said.

I hung up the useless phone . . . just as the power went out and the girls and I found ourselves in darkness.

# CHAPTER 13

## Jessi

Wednesday Evening

I spent the night at my ballet school. That was pretty unusual. Spending the night at any school is unusual, I guess, but I was stuck at dance school with a bunch of teachers and kids I didn't know terribly well.

A lot of the little kids were scared. Their sense of time is different from older kids' or from adults'. If you

say, "You'll see your dad and mom tomorrow;" they understand the concept (you know, like, you'll see them "later"), but "later" could be in a day or a decade.
Plus, I was worried about Quint, but as it turned out, I didn't need to be.

No parent ever showed up that night. Not one.

The phone rang off the hook, though.

People kept calling and calling. "We just can't make it," they'd say. "The storm took us by surprise. I don't know what to do."

The teachers told them not to worry. "*All* the children are here," they'd say. "And we're happy to stay with them. There's food in the kitchen. We'll be fine until tomorrow."

I can't say that I'd been hoping for an adventure, but I seemed to have found one. Personally, I thought Quint's visit would be enough of an adventure. But now I was going to be staying at school, sleeping on my coat and eating Lipton's Cup-O-Noodles soup.

I would be warm, dry, and full — which was more than I could say about Quint. I didn't even know where he *was*.

"Worrying doesn't help anything," Mama always says.

But the more I thought about Quint, the more worries I invented.

What was he doing? Freezing at the train station? Looking around frantically for my father? Maybe he had phoned my house — if he'd brought our number with him, and if he had the proper amount of change. That would be the smart thing to do. In fact, it was what *I* should do.

I was not the only person who wanted to use the phone in the school office, however. I joined a line of about eight kids who were waiting to make calls. The little girl in front of me, who was about seven years old, was crying quietly. So quietly, in fact, that the teachers hadn't noticed she was crying. Their hands were full taking care of the children who were crying noisily.

"Hey, what's the matter?" I asked the girl. She shook her head. A large tear trickled down her cheek. "Are you Holly?" I asked, groping for the name I thought I remembered Mme Noelle using earlier.

"Yes," Holly said, and sniffled. "You're Jessi, right?"

"Right. How come you're crying?"

Holly's lower lip trembled. "Because I don't want to spend the night here. I want my mommy and daddy. And Christopher. And Tattoo. He's our collie dog. And Caboose, my baby doll."

"Your doll's name is Caboose?"

"Yes. And I always sleep with Caboose. Every night."

"But we are going to have a sleepover adventure here at school."

"I don't want to sleep here. I never slept here before."

"Pretend it's a hotel."

"I never slept in a hotel, either."

"Have you ever slept away from home?" I asked.

"No," said Holly with a sob.

Uh-oh. This was not a great situation. I took Holly's hand and squeezed it. Then I held onto it. "I'll stay with you until you talk to your parents, okay? You can pretend I'm your . . ." Hmm. Her what?

"My big sister?" Holly suggested.

"Right!" I grinned. "Your big sister."

The line for the phone moved like a turtle. A sleepy turtle. Mme Duprès was overseeing things, and she tried to limit conversations to three minutes, but the little kids were scared and didn't want to say good-bye to their parents.

At long last, the boy in front of Holly hung up the phone. Holly stepped over to it. She dialed her number with her left hand, since her right hand was busy holding onto *my* hand.

"Hi, Mommy?" Holly said, and burst into tears.

I felt bad for Holly's mother. How awful to get a call from a crying child and not be able to "make it all better."

"*Please* come and get me," Holly kept begging.

After three minutes, Mme Duprès tapped Holly gently on the shoulder. Holly managed to hang up the phone. She looked at me. "Mommy and Daddy can't come. The roads are too dangerous. That's what they said."

I nodded. "I'm sorry, Holly. Hey, do you want to stay with me while I call *my* parents? I might need you."

"Okay." Holly kept a grip on my hand.

I dialed home. *Buzz-buzz-buzz.* Darn. The

phone was busy. I glanced at the line of kids behind me, still waiting to call their families. "Can I try once more?" I asked Mme Duprès. "It was busy."

She gave me permission, and I dialed again. Busy.

"Okay, thanks," I mumbled. I left the office, Holly still attached to me.

Until then, I had been able to convince myself that Quint would call my parents, find out Daddy couldn't pick him up, and then . . . ? Then what? I asked myself. Quint would turn around and go home? (If the trains were still operating.) Surely, Quint had called his own parents. That was it! I should telephone Quint's family in New York.

But what if they *hadn't* heard from him? What if they were assuming Daddy had picked up Quint and me as planned, and we were all safe at home, enjoying the blizzard from in front of our fireplace? I didn't want to worry them. But *I* was worried. *I* needed to know where Quint was and that he was safe.

"Jessi? What are you thinking about?" asked Holly. "You look sad."

"Oh. I'm not sad, really. Just a little worried."

"Why?"

I explained to Holly, as simply as I could,

about Quint and the train and Daddy. "So I'm not sure where Quint is," I finished up. "I mean, he's probably at the station, but I'm not sure."

"Why don't you call the station?" asked Holly. "Maybe somebody could go, 'Quint, Quint!' over the loudspeaker. They could say, 'You have a call from Jessi. Please go to a red circus phone,' or whatever it's called."

"Courtesy phone," I supplied. "Hey, that's a good idea, Holly. I could ask someone to page Quint for me. Then I could talk to him myself."

But I'd already had a turn on the phone. I would have to wait awhile for another.

Holly and I wandered back to the room in which we'd held our rehearsal that afternoon. Two teachers were there, along with a group of the youngest kids.

Most of the kids were about Holly's age. Several were crying. The teachers were trying to comfort the kids, but they couldn't deal with all of them at the same time.

I guess taking care of children comes naturally to me, what with Becca and Squirt and my baby-sitting jobs. Holly and I approached the nearest crying kid, a little boy with huge brown eyes.

"Do you know who this is?" I asked Holly.

She nodded. "Yup. That's Gianmarco. He plays a mouse."

"Hi, Gianmarco," I said. "I'm Jessi. You probably aren't used to seeing me in my regular clothes. I play the Mouse King."

"Oh." Gianmarco wouldn't look at me.

"Are you worried about your parents?" I asked.

"My dad." Gianmarco bit his lower lip.

"You know what? My dad couldn't pick me up, either," I told him. "A lot of moms and dads decided not to drive in the snow. Trust me, they're safer at home."

"But what about us?" wailed Gianmarco.

"Yeah, what about us?" Holly chimed in.

"We're going to stay right here and have a wonderful time. It'll be like a big party. Hey, look!" I pointed across the room. "Here comes dinner." The school secretary was struggling through the doorway with a tray of paper cups, plastic spoons, packages of instant soup and dried food, and a plate of cookies left from a party the teachers had held recently.

"Where are we going to eat?" asked Holly.

"Well, we're going to eat, um," I paused, "right here on the floor. We'll have a picnic. Okay, you guys? Let's find our coats, spread them on the floor, and sit on them. We'll pretend they're one big blanket, and we're at a picnic in the country. . . . Mmm, I think I smell hot dogs!"

"I smell pizza!" cried Gianmarco.

He and Holly and I sat on the floor, eating instant soup and butter cookies.

"Simply delicious hamburgers," commented Holly.

"Awesome ice cream sundae," added another voice.

One by one the children were joining our imaginary picnic.

Mme Noelle peeked in the room and smiled gratefully at me.

Twenty minutes later, the children were calmer. Some of them seemed to be enjoying the adventure. I decided to try calling Quint at the train station.

I stood up. "I'll be right back," I said to Holly.

But she wasn't listening to me. She was staring at the doorway to the room. "Who is that?" she whispered.

I turned around. In the doorway stood . . . Quint.

I ran to him and threw my arms around him. He was snow-covered and frozen, but he seemed fine. "How did you get here?" I cried.

"I walked," Quint replied through chattering teeth. "When your dad didn't show up, I figured he couldn't drive in the snow. So I asked a guy at the train station for directions to the dance school. And here I am."

I hardly dared to believe what was happening. But after a few moments, I came to my senses. "We have to call my parents — and yours — and tell them where you are," I said.

I led Quint into the office. When we picked up the receiver, we discovered the phone had gone dead.

# CHAPTER 14

## Mary Anne

Wednesday Evening

Our overnight sitting job turned into even more of an adventure than Mallory and I had expected. First came the snow, then came the phone call from Mr. and Mrs. Pike. Oh, the Abominable Snowman caused some excitement, too....

"The Abominable Snowman?" Claire repeated. She gave Adam a hard look. "He steals homework? Then, does that mean he comes into houses?"

"Of course," Adam replied. "What did you think? That he steals homework from teachers? That's no fun. He has to steal homework *before* kids hand it in to their teachers. Then he yells at them, 'Do it over!' "

"Does he come into your *room?*" Claire persisted.

"Depends on where your homework is. If it's in your school locker, he goes in your locker. If it's at home he goes in your bedroom."

I could see Claire forming another question. She was about to ask it when the phone rang. Instead she dove for the phone. "Hi, Mommy!" she exlaimed when she'd answered it. "It's snowing!"

Claire told Mrs. Pike how the day had gone. Then she handed the phone to Mallory. "Mommy wants to talk to you," she said.

Mallory took the phone. She listened, her face growing more and more serious. She kept saying. "Mm-hmm, mm-hmm."

"What?" Jordan whispered, elbowing Mallory. "What's Mom saying?"

Mal shrugged him off and turned to face the wall. "Mm-hmm, mm-hmm. . . . Okay, hang on a sec. Mary Anne, Mom wants to talk to you now."

"Hi, Mrs. Pike," I said, cradling the receiver between my ear and shoulder.

"Hi, Mary Anne. Listen, it's snowing in New York, too, and the trains have stopped running. We aren't going to be able to get home tonight."

"Wow," I whispered. "Um, okay. Well, we'll be all right."

"This is a big responsibility," said Mrs. Pike.

"I know, but like I said, my dad's at home. And Mrs. Barrett. And Mrs. McGill."

"Right. Listen, will you and Mallory tell the others that we'll see them tomorrow? Oh, and we're staying with the Sombergs.' We gave you their number before we left. Call if you need to. Otherwise, we'll talk in the morning. I'll phone you when we know what our plans are."

"Okay," I agreed.

We hung up. I was slightly nervous about telling the younger Pike kids that their parents wouldn't be home until the next day — but the kids didn't care.

"We'll be pioneers!" exclaimed Margo. "Snow pioneers."

And Nicky jumped around crying, "No school, no parents! No school, no parents!"

"It's a shame he's so broken up about it," Mal whispered to me.

I giggled. "I better call my dad," I said then. "He should know what's going on. I'll call Mrs. Barrett, too."

"Thanks," said Mallory. "I'll try to settle the kids down."

"Hello, Dad?" I said a few moments later. "Guess what." I explained the situation to him. I must have sounded awfully calm, because instead of getting hysterical and crying out "I'll be right over!" he just said, "Do you want me to come over, honey?"

"I think we're okay," I replied. "We wouldn't have seen Mr. and Mrs. Pike until tomorrow, even if they had come home on time."

"All right. Just as well. I haven't heard from Sharon and I'd like to be here if she calls. I want to know that she and Dawn reached the airport safely."

"Okay. I'm going to call Mrs. Barrett now, just so she knows we're on our own here tonight. I'll talk to you later this evening."

" 'Night, honey."

" 'Night, Dad."

I called Mrs. Barrett as I'd planned. Then I

decided to phone Stacey. It couldn't hurt to let her and her mom know what Mal and I were up to.

I glanced out the kitchen window. The Pikes' back windows face the McGills' back windows, across their yards.

Funny, I thought. Stacey's house was dark. Had she and her mom already gone to bed? It wasn't likely. I tried to remember if their lights had been on when Mal and the kids and I were playing in the snow, but I couldn't. I hesitated, then dialed Stacey's number, praying I wouldn't wake her or her mother.

*Ring, ring, ring, ring. . . .* The phone eventually rang seven times before I decided no one was going to answer it.

I hung up. "Hey, Mal!" I called.

"Yeah?"

I found the kids in the rec room, sacked out in front of the TV. "Mal, no one's home at Stacey's. Isn't that weird?"

"Kind of. Maybe they got stuck somewhere when the snow came. Like at a friend's house. What was Stacey doing this afternoon?"

"I'm not sure." I tried to picture the appointment pages from the BSC notebook. Had Stacey been scheduled for a sitting job? I didn't think so.

134

"Oh, well. Wherever they are, I'm sure they're fine," said Mal.

"Yeah."

"Mal?" spoke up Byron. "I'm hungry."

"But you just had hot chocolate. And before that, you had dinner."

"I'm still hungry."

"Me, too," said Nicky and Vanessa.

Mal heaved a sigh. "I'll go see what there is," she said, and disappeared upstairs. "Hey, Mary Anne! Come here!" she called a minute later.

I ran to the kitchen. "What?" I asked.

"I just realized something. We have practically no food."

"You're kidding."

"Nope. Mom left enough for breakfast today and tomorrow, and for tonight's dinner, but then she was going to do a major grocery shopping when she got home tomorrow. She didn't even have stuff for our lunches, remember?"

"But you must have *some* food," I said, frowning.

"Oh, yeah. We have plenty of flour and sugar and coffee and frosting mix. And I think I saw a couple of TV dinners in the freezer. But we're nearly out of milk, eggs, cereal, juice, fruit, bread — "

"Okay, I get the picture," I interrupted.

"So what are we going to do tomorrow if Mom and Dad don't get home and we can't leave the house?"

"Well, we won't starve. Trust me. We'll borrow stuff from the Barretts. We'll eat frosting if we have to."

"Hey, I just thought of something!" exclaimed Mal. "How much emergency money did Mom give us?"

"A lot," I replied.

"Enought to order in a couple of pizzas?"

"Definitely. If the trucks can make deliveries, we're all set. Want to call Pizza Express?"

"As quickly as possible," replied Mallory.

"Okay." I picked up the phone and held it to my ear. I shook the receiver.

"What's wrong?" asked Mal.

"The phone's not working."

"Huh. That's wei — Hey!"

We had been standing in the kitchen, talking, and now we couldn't see a thing. Not even our hands. The house was in total darkness.

"Help!" yelled Margo from the rec room.

That was followed by the sound of Claire crying.

"The TV is off!" shouted Adam.

I thought the house seemed awfully quiet.

136

Now I knew why. The power was out, as well as the phone. *Nothing* was working, not the TV, not the radios, not the refrigerator, not the stereo.

Mal and I spent the next few minutes calming Clair and Margo, hunting up flashlights, and trying to remember which appliances had been on so we could turn them off. We had just switched off the television when a horrible thought occurred to me.

*What if the heat didn't work? We could freeze to death.*

The heat did work, though. It was practically the only thing that did.

"Thank goodness," I murmured.

Mal, her brothers and sisters, and I crowded onto a couple of couches in the rec room. We had found three flashlights, and they were turned on. Our faces looked ghostly in the dark house.

"Hey, Claire," said Adam. "Did I mention that the Abominable Snowman likes darkness?"

"Yipes!" shrieked Claire.

# CHAPTER 15

## Dawn

Wednesday Evening

Wednesday night was one of the longest in my life. Somehow, it even seemed longer than the nights when Claud and I were stranded on that island after the boat wreck. For one thing, there's nothing like sleeping in a hard plastic chair. For another, there's nothing like sleeping in a hard plastic chair with about twenty-five other people who are doing the same thing.

Guess what Mom and I found when we reached Jeff's gate at the airport.

A smiling and relieved Jeff? No.

An anxious and hysterical Jeff? No.

Pandemonium? Well, almost.

A bunch of people were crowded around the ticket counter. An agent from the airline was trying to talk to them, but they were making so much noise they couldn't hear what he was saying.

I glanced at Mom. "This doesn't look good," I said.

Mom strode to the counter and joined the crowd. Since no one would quiet down, the agent gave up trying to speak. He started to leave the counter. *Then* everybody shut up.

The man, looking annoyed, said, "Thank you. As I said a moment ago, the flight from Los Angeles has been delayed. Currently, the scheduled arrival time is about an hour from now. I'll keep you updated periodically and will let you know quickly if there's a change in plans."

"Mom!" I exclaimed. "Jeff isn't here yet!" What a relief. That meant he wasn't wandering around feeling abandoned.

"Right." Mom smiled.

"It's a good thing he doesn't get airsick,

though. The plane's probably circling. Imagine circling for an hour."

My mother made a face. "I was once on a plane that circled for two hours. I thought I would die!"

"Well . . . what should we do? We have an hour to kill," I pointed out.

"There's always food," Mom suggested.

"Yeah. But we just ate dinner. Besides, do you really think we'll find healthy food in an airport, the capital of bad sandwiches?"

"You never know," said Mom, smiling again. "Anyway, let's wander around. We'll look in the gift shop and the newsstand."

"Okay."

The terminal was boiling hot, so we took off our coats and carried them to the gift shop. Here's the thing about the gift shop. Nearly every item on sale has the word "Connecticut" written on it. There are racks of Connecticut sweat shirts and T-shirts and windbreakers, shelves of Connecticut caps and visors, and display case after display case of Connecticut salt and pepper shakers, spoon rests, snow globes, plaques, bumper stickers, pencil cases, key chains, refrigerator magnets, paper-weights, pens, piggy banks, plates, mugs, you name it.

"Hey, Mom," I said. "If your plane landed

at this airport and for some reason you weren't sure what state you were in, do you think you could figure it out by coming into this store?''

Mom frowned, and pretended to look all around her. At last she said, "Nah.''

We looked in the newsstand next, which is more like a store than a stand. And it carried paperback books, too. I bet you could find a copy of any magazine in the country there. I leafed through a magazine about California. I read an entire article. Then I checked my watch. Half an hour had gone by.

A cold feeling washed over me.

"Mom!'' I said with a gasp. I thrust the magazine back onto the stand. "I just thought of something.''

My mother must have seen the panic in my face. "What?''she exclaimed.

"Jeff's probably going crazy on the plane. I was relieved when the guy said the plane hadn't landed yet. But Jeff's probably scared anyway. Maybe he's wondering whether we'll wait for him. Also, when he does land, how are we going to get home? It's still snowing.''

"Dawn, you are picking up Mary Anne's one bad habit, which is worrying too much. We can't do anything now except wait. I hope Jeff knows we wouldn't turn around and leave the airport without him. And as for the snow,

I don't know. Maybe by the time Jeff arrives, it will have let up. I won't do anything foolish."

"I know you won't," I said. "Sorry."

Mom gave me a hug. "You don't have to apologize," she said.

She paid for a copy of *The New York Times*, and we returned to Jeff's gate. We sat in these awful, hard plastic chairs. They were the chairs I mentioned earlier that were so, so uncomfortable. You know, Claud and I really did get stranded on an island once. Not a desert island, just a small island off the coast of Connecticut. We'd been out sailing, a storm had blown up, one of our boats was wrecked, and we washed ashore on the island, where we stayed until we were rescued a few days later.

"May I have your attention, please?" The airline official was speaking into a mike at the ticket counter again. Guess what he announced this time. He announced that Jeff's plane would not be arriving at *all* that night. It had been rerouted to Washington, D.C., because of the snow (which apparently Washington was not getting).

"Washington?!" I shrieked to my mother. "But Jeff — "

"Hold on a sec," said Mom, cutting me off.

"I'll go talk to the agent. You stay here and watch our coats, please."

I bit my nails as I watched Mom hurry to the counter and try to talk to the guy. Needless to say, she was not the only one doing that. So several minutes passed before she returned to her seat.

"What'd he say?" I asked.

"Just what he said before. The plane can't land because of the snow, so it's being re-routed to Washington, which is getting a little rain but nothing else. It can land safely there."

"But how's Jeff going to get *here*?" I cried.

"The man said the passengers will be flown to Connecticut tomorrow morning, if the weather has improved and the runway is clear enough."

"Tomorrow! What's Jeff going to do all night?"

"One of the flight attendants will take care of him. Everyone is being put up at a hotel until the morning. The attendant will make sure Jeff gets from the airport to the hotel and back to the airport tomorrow."

Mom sounded much more assured than she looked.

"What do we do now?" I asked.

"Wait around to see if anything changes."

# Dawn

My mother and I sat quietly for awhile. Mom tried to read her newspaper, but I don't think she was having any success. She never turned a page. And she jumped a mile when the airline guy announced that anyone who needed to do so could make a free phone call to Washington to try to contact the friends or relatives who'd been stranded there.

My mother dashed to the counter. She was the fourth person in line to use the telephone. But she never got a chance. The person in front of her was chattering away when suddenly he stopped. Then he said, "Hello? Hello? . . . HELLO?" He turned to the man at the desk. "The phone just went dead," he informed him.

The man pressed a few buttons, trying to get another line. But it was no use. *All* the phones at the airport were out of order.

"Lines must be down," someone said.

"They *can't* be," I replied.

"Attention, please," began a voice, speaking over the paging system. "Unfortunately, I must tell you that the airport is now being closed due to the storm. There will be no more incoming or outgoing flights until further notice. We do not advise leaving the airport to drive anywhere. If you have questions, please ask someone connected with your airline. Thank you."

"Mo-*om!* We're *stuck* here," I exclaimed.

"I know. And now I can't call Richard to let him know where we are. I hope the airport closing makes the news, and he figures out what must have happened and assumes we're safe."

I felt the way I did when Claud and I were stranded on the island. We had had to make the best of things then, hoping that soon we'd be with the people we love and that their worrying would be over. So Mom and I settled in for a night at the airport. Since it was still fairly early, we went first to the snack bar, which was going to stay open all night, serving food — and free coffee and sodas. We discovered that the capital of bad sandwiches featured surprisingly good salads. After we'd eaten, we went to the newsstand. Mom bought each of us a book, which we took back to the waiting room. Then we tried to get comfortable in those chairs. This just was not possible. We couldn't stretch out. Every time I moved, my spine mashed into the armrest or the back or something. Finally I curled into a ball, rested my head on my coat, and tried to read.

# CHAPTER 16

## Stacey

Wednesday Evening

I'm not sure when I've been more scared. I mean, I really can't think of anything worse than that moment when Mom and I realized we were stuck in the snow and dark in the middle of who knows where, and would probably be there all night. What about the heat? I worried. If it stopped working, could we freeze to death in a few hours? How fast did that happen? Could we get frostbite and lose our fingers and toes?

Those were the things I was worrying about. Mom was worrying about something else: my diabetes.

$\Lambda$t first, the thought that we were in great danger was so stunning that my mom and I couldn't even talk to each other. We sat stiffly in our seats. Mom left the car running so the heater and the headlights could stay on. I tried desperately to figure out where we were and then realized it didn't matter. Unless we were *positive* we were near a house or some sort of shelter, we would be foolish to try to walk anywhere.

I gazed out the window. The sky continued to fling handfuls of snow onto our car. It wasn't even pretty. It was wild and angry and unreasonable.

Mom turned in her seat and sighed, the first sound either of us had made in more than ten minutes. "I'm sorry, honey," she said.

"Hey, this isn't your fault," I replied. But then I couldn't help adding, "Mom, what happens if the heater stops working?"

"We'll stay as close together as we can. For body heat."

"But can you freeze to death overnight?"

"I don't know. I suppose so."

After a long silence I said, "Um, I hate to say this, but I'm hungry."

Mom clapped her hand to her forehead. "What on earth was I thinking?" she ex-

claimed. "You need to eat. And your insulin. Do you have — "

"My injection kit is with me," I told her. "I never go anywhere without it. But tonight will be the first time I've had to use it because of an actual emergency."

"What about food?" pressed Mom.

"Well, there's the rest of the snack I brought — some carrot sticks and crackers — but I don't know how long that will hold me. Do you have *any* food with you, Mom?"

"Lifesavers. That's it."

I ate the carrots and crackers.

"Feel better?" Mom asked.

"Sort of," I replied. "But I should be eating dinner now. I need it."

"I know." Mom put her hand on the horn and nearly blasted my head off with the sound.

"Mom! Stop!" I yelped.

"I'm trying to attract attention," she replied, pausing for a moment. "If any houses are around here, maybe someone will hear us."

"And arrest you for disturbing the peace?"

Finally I got a smile out of Mom. "Jail would be warmer than our car," she said. "And I bet there's coffee in jail."

"Mom? What made you fall in love with Dad?" I asked suddenly. The question took me by as much surprise as it took my mother.

"Stace. What a time to ask that," said Mom.

"I want to know."

"Right this second?"

"Do you have anything better to do?"

"I guess not."

"So?"

Mom looked thoughtful. "What makes anyone fall in love with anyone else?" was her response. She spread her hands in her lap, and I noticed that she no longer wore her wedding band. When had she taken it off?

I waited for Mom to answer her own question, since *I* didn't have an answer. When she didn't, I said, "I give up. What?"

Mom shook her head, smiling. "That was a rhetorical question, Stace. It didn't call for an answer."

"*My* question wasn't rhetorical. I'm serious. I'm only thirteen. I haven't fallen in love yet. And I want to know what made you fall in love with Dad. This could be an important piece of information."

"Okay. Let me see." Mom paused. "Well," she began, "the first time I can remember thinking I was in love was when I realized your father and I had so many common likes and dislikes that it was as if one of us had been cloned from the other. It seemed that every day we'd discover something new. Not only did we both love the old *I Love Lucy* show, but we shared the same favorite episode. In case you're wondering, it's the one in which Lucy decides Ricky needs some publicity. So she poses as royalty from a made-up country — the Maharincess of Franistan — and arranges a special meeting with Ricky Ricardo, her singing idol."

I giggled. "What else, Mom?"

"Oh, other silly things. Our favorite brand of jeans was Levi's. Our favorite kind of music was swing. Our favorite bandleader was Tommy Dorsey. And we couldn't stand cigarettes. Neither of us had ever smoked one. . . . Honey? What's the matter? Oh, I *told* you this was going to be hard to explain."

"What? It's not that, Mom. Honest. Believe it or not, you were making sense."

"Thanks a lot!"

"You know what I mean. Anyway, it's just that, um, I don't think the heat's on anymore. I can't feel it coming out of the vents."

Mom removed one of her gloves and held her bare hand first to one vent, then to another. She fiddled with the control for the heat and tested the vents again. "You're right," she said at last. It isn't working." My mother sank back, resting her head against the seat cushion.

"I think we'll be warm for awhile," I said, trying to sound positive. "The heat has *been* on ever since we left the mall."

Mom sat forward suddenly and rammed her hand on the horn again. The sound blasted through the darkness. She stopped after a few seconds, opened her window a crack, and yelled outside, "HELP! HELP!"

I joined her with a long wail out my side of the car. "HE-E-E-E-E-E-E-E-LP."

*Honk, honk, ho-o-o-o-o-onk.*

"Help, help, he-e-e-e-e-e-lp!"

Of course, nothing happened. Who did we think was going to answer us? The trees?

When we'd calmed down, Mom said, "I think I'll try to move the car again."

"Are you sure you should open the door and go outside? You'll let cold air in," I told her.

"I don't know," replied Mom, and then she burst into laughter.

"What's so funny?"

"We're out of gas," she said, giggling helplessly. "I just noticed. I took a look at the gas gauge. It's on Empty. I guess we won't be going *any*where tonight." Mom dabbed tears from her eyes.

"Gee, that's hysterical," I said. And then it occurred to me that *Mom* might be hysterical. "Well, tomorrow we'll leave the car and walk until we find help," I said sensibly. "I bet the storm will be over by then. We'll just walk back to the highway and find a gas station or a diner or something."

"Right."

"I think I'll try to go to sleep," I said. I didn't know what else to do. I couldn't stand to watch my mother anymore, though.

I closed my eyes.

"Hey!" cried Mom.

"What?" I snapped. I wanted her to leave me alone.

"Someone's coming!" Mom was looking in the rearview mirror. "I see headlights behind us." Mom leaned on the horn. She blinked our own headlights on and off. And several moments later, a station wagon eased to a stop next to our car. A man got out and walked around to Mom's window.

"Mom! You have no idea who he is!" I cried. "He could be a desperate criminal! I feel like we're in one of those horror stories they tell at overnight camp. For all you know, he just escaped from prison."

Mom rolled down her window.

"You folks need some help?" asked the man.

"I'll say," replied Mom. "We're stuck. We're out of gas and our heater isn't working. I don't even know where we are."

"My wife and I live just down the road," said the man. "You're welcome to spend the night with us."

Mom turned to me with raised eyebrows.

# CHAPTER 17

## Mallory

Wednesday Night
and Thursday Morning

I said I was looking forward to a baby-sitting adventure, but this was a little more than I had had in mind. Now I understand what my father means when he says, "Be careful what you wish for. You might get it." We got an adventure all right -- a blizzard, a power failure, the phone lines down, a food semi-emergency, and an unexpected late-night visitor.

"That's enough about the Abominable Snowman, Adam, I said. "And I mean it. Claire, there is no such thing as an Abominable Snowman."

"Are you sure?" she asked. She was sitting in my lap, holding a flashlight in one hand. The thumb from her other hand was in her mouth. She was talking around it. *And* playing with her hair. I have never seen a five-year-old do so many things at the same time.

"I am positive," I replied.

"I'm still hungry," said Byron.

"I'm scared," said Margo.

"I'm tired of sitting here," said Jordan.

"Let's sing a song," said Claire, whose thumb was still in her mouth. "We sang a good one in school today." She belted out, *Head, shoulders, knees and toes, knees and toes. Head, shoulders, knees and toes, knees and toes. Eyes and ears and nose and mouth and chin. Head, shoulders, knees and toes, knees and toes."* As Claire mentioned each part of her body, she pointed to it with the flashlight. Then she cried, "Everybody!"

Mary Anne, Margo, and I joined in. We sang one more chorus. When we paused, Byron said, "My stomach is rumbling."

"We have to conserve food," I informed him.

"How can we?" he replied. "The electricity's off. Everything in the refrigerator and the freezer is going to spoil."

Uh-oh. Mary Anne and I hadn't thought of that.

"I know!" Byron went on. "We can have a picnic! We'll eat up all the stuff that will melt or go bad. We better start with the ice cream."

"Actually," said Mary Anne, "that isn't a bad idea. We don't know when the power will come back. If it's out all night, a lot of food *will* get spoiled. We might as well eat some of it."

Vanessa looked wary. "There are frozen vegetables in the freezer," she said hesitatingly. "We don't have to eat those, do we?" And then she added, "Carrots and corn and broccoli and beans, you must know that to me this means, um, this means — "

"It means we don't eat most of the stuff in the freezer," supplied Jordan. "Come on, you guys. Forget the vegetables. Let's find the ice cream!"

My brothers and sisters thundered upstairs, guided by their flashlights. Nicky opened the freezer and Adam pulled out two half-eaten containers of ice cream. "Mint chocolate chip and butter pecan. Let's start with these," he said.

Vanessa aimed a flashlight into the freezer. "There are the vegetables," she said. "I'll just stick them in back."

Byron, Adam, Jordan, Vanessa, Nicky, Margo, and Claire crowded around the table with spoons and dug into the containers, without benefit of bowls.

"You'd think they'd been raised by wolves," I whispered to Mary Anne.

She smiled. Then she said, "You know, since we can't get hold of Pizza Express, which probably isn't delivering anyway, and as long as the kids are eating, maybe you and I should look around and gather up food that *won't* go bad. We should say it's off-limits until tomorrow."

"Good idea," I agreed.

While the kids pigged out, Mary Anne and I collected nearly empty boxes of cereal, the ends of loaves of bread, several apples, and so on. I was rummaging through a cabinet where I thought Mom had stuck a box of crackers when . . .

. . . the doorbell rang.

"It's the Abominable Snowman!" shrieked Claire.

"It is?" Adam shrieked back. Then he caught himself. "The Abominable Snowman doesn't bother with doorbells," he said.

"Do robbers?" asked Vanessa.

"I don't think so," I answered uncertainly.

"But who could be out in this weather?" asked Mary Anne. "And at this hour? It's getting kind of late."

"Should we answer the door?" said Nicky, hopping from one foot to the other.

"Someone might need help," I pointed out.

"You guys stay in the kitchen," Mary Anne said to my brothers and sisters. "Mal and I will see who's at the door."

Mary Anne and I tiptoed through the front hallway. We peered out the small windows by the door. "I can't make out anything," I said.

"Wait a second, I can see," said Mary Anne. (She wears glasses just for reading. I have to wear them all the time. My vision is about as good as a mole's. Even when my glasses are on.) "It's my dad!" Mary Anne exclaimed.

"Your dad? Are you positive?"

"Yup." Mary Anne opened the door.

Sure enough, standing on the stoop was her father. "I hope I didn't scare you," he said.

"Oh, no," I replied. (My heart was tap dancing in my chest.)

"I just wanted to make sure you're all right.

160

I was a bit nervous when the lights went out and I couldn't phone you."

"We're fine, Dad," said Mary Anne. "Honest." She told him what my brothers and sisters were doing. "We're going to go to bed soon," she added.

"All right. I'd offer to stay with you, but Sharon isn't back yet and I didn't hear from her before the telephones went out, so I'm a little worried. But I suppose no news is good news."

"Gosh," I said as Mr. Spier stepped carefully down our icy front stoop. "Your mom and Dawn aren't back yet, and we don't know where Stacey and *her* mom are. It's kind of spooky, isn't it? I wonder what our other friends are doing."

"Boy, I wish I knew," replied Mary Anne.

An hour later, Mary Anne and I had succeeded in putting my brothers and sisters to bed. It was quite late — long past their bedtime — but I didn't care. We wouldn't have school the next day, so we could sleep in.

I lay cozily in my warm bed that night. Even so, I didn't sleep much. Probably the sugar from the ice cream and hot chocolate. Also, I couldn't help worrying about Stacey and Dawn. I was driven crazy by the fact that I was unable to phone them, or anyone else. Had Jessi and Quint made it back from Stoneybrook or were they stuck somewhere? Was Quint even in Connecticut?

I listened to the wind whistle around the eaves of the house.

Twice, I tiptoed to the window and peeked outside. Not a light anywhere. Not even a streetlight. The power had not been turned on. I squinted my eyes and tried to see what the blizzard was doing. I was pretty sure snow was still falling, because the plows had not yet come down our street.

Around two o'clock I fell asleep. But I awoke again before six. I peeped out the window. Day was breaking, so I could finally see. It was snowing, but only lightly, and I thought the sky looked brighter than it had on Wednesday afternoon. I tried to guess how much snow had fallen and decided on at least two feet. Cars were half buried, our stoop was a small hill of snow (Mr. Spier's footprints had vanished), and shrubbery was completely buried.

I wondered if the power was back yet, and I turned on the radio alarm clock. A newscaster was saying, "All public, private, and parochial schools are *closed* today."

Yes! No school — and the electricity had returned.

I switched off the clock before the radio could waken Mary Anne or Vanessa. Then I tiptoed downstairs and double-checked the appliances. The only thing on that should have been off was a light in the rec room, so I flipped its switch, then tiptoed back upstairs and checked on the boys and Claire and Margo. They were sleeping peacefully.

I returned to my own bed.

"Mal?" mumbled Mary Anne from her cot.

"Yeah?"

"What's going on?"

"I think the storm is over. Oh, and school's closed."

# CHAPTER 18

## Claudia

Wednesday Night and
Thursday Morning

Waht an evning. Chewy was missing and the phones werent working and the electricy was out. I was'nt sure which was the whorst. Of corse, Chewy's disappearance was awful. But I needed the phone to call for help. And electricty would have been nice while I was searching for him. Try finding a black dog in the pitch dark! But I did my best that night and by the nest day I felt pretty proud of myself.

"Hey! Who turned out the lights?" called Myriah.

"Yeah, who turned them out?" echoed Gabbie.

"Nobody," I replied.

"Mr. Nobody?'!" yelped Gabbie.

"No. I mean, nobody turned them out. I think the snow knocked down some power lines. We probably don't have any electricity at all. Myriah, do you know where your mom and dad keep their flashlight?"

"Yes. It's in the cabinet in the rec room. And it's *big*. It needs lots of batteries."

We felt our way through a hall and into the rec room. "Which cabinet?" I asked Myriah. (She and Gabbie were holding onto me by my belt loops.)

"This one, I think," she replied.

I opened the cabinet and reached one hand inside. Since I couldn't see a *thing*, I suddenly became afraid of all sorts of awful creatures that might be hiding there, just waiting for my hand to appear . . . then *snap!* But the first object I touched felt like a flashlight, so I took it out of the cabinet, fumbled for the switch, found it, pressed it up, and —

Okay. We had light. Now what?

"*There* you are! exclaimed Gabbie. "And

there's Myriah, and here I am!" She sounded amazed.

Okay. We had light. Now what? Put the girls to bed? Continue my search for Chewy? I decided the girls were my first priority, so I guided them carefully upstairs to their bedrooms. They did not like getting ready for bed in the dark, and I couldn't blame them.

"This is scary," whispered Gabbie.

She was right.

"I don't like walking around corners," said Myriah.

Neither did I.

Nevertheless, I thought I was actually going to get the girls to sleep without problems, until Myriah said, "What if we have to get up during the night? We won't be able to see. Even the night-light in the bathroom doesn't work."

Uh-oh. Good point.

"Well, I need the flashlight for a little while longer. Until I go to bed," I said. "Then I could put it in the hallway or the bathroom and leave it on. How would that be?" I asked, already praying that the batteries wouldn't run out.

"Okay," said Myriah. "Thank you."

"Okay, thank you," said Gabbie.

"Into bed, then," I told the girls. "You're up a little late tonight."

"I never went to bed in the dark before," said Gabbie.

"Hmm. Why don't you pretend you're going to bed and the light is on as usual?" I suggested. (Gabbie climbed into her bed.) "Now close your eyes," I said. (Gabbie closed them.) "Now open them." (Gabbie opened them.) "See? I just turned off the light!"

Gabbie giggled.

"Turn off *my* light!" cried Myriah.

"Okay." I led Myriah into her room and put her to bed. "I'll be back upstairs in awhile," I said. "I'm going to sleep in your room, remember? In the other bed? And I'll set the flashlight in the hall first."

Myriah smiled. (Or at least I think she did.) As I left her room, she called after me in a loud whisper, "Good luck with Chewy!"

Now how did she know I planned to continue the search?

"Thanks," I replied.

I carried the heavy flashlight down the steps to the first floor. Once again, I walked from room to room, softly calling, "Chewy! Chewy! Here, boy! Chewy, where are you?" And once again I found nothing. Well, not *nothing*. I found a cat toy under the couch and a mitten behind a door. In the front hallway, I found a letter that had fallen behind a table.

And then I heard footsteps.

I heard footsteps *outside*, padding closer and closer to the —

*Ding-dong!*

"Oh, my lord!" I shrieked.

"Honey?" called a muffled voice from the other side of the door. "Is that you, Claudia? It's Mom."

"Mom?" I called back. "Really?"

"Really. I just wanted to find out if everything was okay."

I opened the door and let her inside. "Mom!" I cried, as if I hadn't seen her in a year or two. "I'm so glad it's you!"

"Are you all right? Did you know the phones went out, too? I thought you might have been trying to call us. Are the girls okay?"

So many questions. I smiled, and my heart, which felt as if it had been beating as fast as a hummingbird's, slowed down a little. "Yeah. We're fine. The girls are asleep. And I did know the phones went out because I tried to call you. Mom, Chewy's missing!"

"Oh, honey. When did you realize he was gone?"

"A little while ago. Myriah and Gabbie wanted to say good night to him, and we couldn't find him. I knew he'd been inside before, because I gave him his dinner. And I'm pretty sure no one let him out, but we've looked everywhere. What if he *is* outside? What if he's caught in this storm somewhere? If he doesn't come back, I will never forgive myself. Poor Chewy. He must be *freezing*."

"Claudia, calm down," said Mom. "I'll help you look through the house again and then we'll call for him outside. That's all we can do. It's much too cold and windy to search outside, and besides, you can barely see through the snow. If we don't find Chewy tonight, I think you'll have to wait until tomorrow to look any further."

That made sense. "Okay," I agreed.

So Mom and I looked and looked, then leaned out the front and back doors and called and called. No Chewy.

"I'll stay with you tonight," said Mom as we sank onto the couch in the playroom. "I can sleep right here."

"Oh, that's okay. Honest," I told her. "This job is my responsibility. I don't want anyone to think I can't handle it. And if I do need you, you're right across the street."

"I imagine that by the time we wake up tomorrow, the power will be on again," said my mother. "Maybe the phones will work, too. You'll feel better then. But I *am* happy to stay here."

"No. Thanks, though. I'll call you first thing in the morning — or I'll bring the girls over for a visit if the phone still doesn't work."

"All right."

Mom left then, and not long afterward, I went to bed and fell fast asleep. But I didn't stay asleep. I kept waking up, wondering what had happened to Chewy. Sometimes I listened for Laura. I wasn't used to being in charge of a baby for so long. But the Perkinses' house remained quiet until just after five o'clock.

That was when I realized that somebody was staring at me. From about two inches away. I was face-to-face with . . . Gabbie.

"Gabbers?" I whispered. "What are you doing up? Are you okay?"

"I hear funny sounds, Claudia," she replied.

"Why don't you sleep in here with Myriah and me for awhile?"

"No. I want to see what the funny sounds are."

I yawned. "Okay," I said, sitting up. "What do the sounds sound like?"

"I don't know."

Gabbie led me to the head of the stairs. I listened. Sure enough. I heard funny sounds,

too. I heard a sort of snuffling and scratch-
ing.

"Gabbie!" I exclaimed. "I think it's Chewy!"

I grabbed the flashlight and we hurried
downstairs. We followed the sounds to the
basement door. When I opened it, out
bounded Chewy.

"Chewbacca!" cried Gabbie.

"Chewy! Have you been in the basement all
night? How did you get shut in there anyway?
And why didn't you answer us when we
called?" (What a question to ask a dog.) "I bet
you have to go to the bathroom, don't you?"
I asked, as Gabbie hugged Chewy tightly. I
threw my coat on over my nightgown, and let
Chewy out the back door. I didn't follow him,
though. I found myself staring at an amazingly
white, fuzzy world. Snow was just about all I
could see. It had blown and drifted against
everything. I had never seen so much snow.

"It's taller than me!" said Gabbie.

It wasn't, but it must have looked that way
to her. Anyway, it was more than half as tall
as she was.

When Chewy came back inside, I dried him
off. I looked at my watch. Not even five-thirty.
But the girls and I were up for the day. Laura
awoke because she needed a diaper change.

Myriah awoke because Chewy ran to her bedroom and gave her slurpy kisses.

We checked the electricity. Working! We checked the phone. Working! We listened to the radio. School was closed!

After I called Mom, I had fun helping the girls get dressed and then making breakfast for them. In the middle of our breakfast, Mr. Perkins phoned, saying that he and Mrs. Perkins would be home as soon as the roads had been cleared.

"Would you like dessert?" I asked Myriah and Gabbie later.

"Dessert after breakfast?" said Myriah.

"Sure. We just had a blizzard. We should make snow cream right away." I showed the girls how to collect clean snow and put a scoop into a bowl. Then I poured maple syrup over each scoop.

"Yummy!" said Myriah.

"Yummy!" said Gabbie.

And soon they headed outdoors to begin creating their snow family.

# CHAPTER 19

## Jessi

Wednesday Night
and Thursday Morning
I was really
proud of Holly and
the other young kids
who spent the night
at our dance school.
They were quite calm,
all things considered.
I'm not sure I
would have handled
myself that well
when I was their
age. Of course, this
doesn't mean there
was no complaining.
There was whining
and complaining, but

*mostly, I think the kids had fun. And so did I!*

Around nine o'clock on Wednesday night, the younger dance students began to grow tired. They squabbled with each other. They spilled things. They whined.

"Sounds like bedtime," I whispered to Quint.

"I'll say," Quint replied.

"Somehow, I had thought we might be home by now," I went on. "I kept thinking the storm would stop suddenly, the plows would come through, and our parents would arrive. I guess not." I was looking out the window. If anything, the snow was coming down even harder.

Quint shook his head. "We're here for the night."

At least the electricity was on. I didn't know that Stoneybrook was without power, so I didn't realize how lucky I was to be stranded in Stamford. All I could see were the problems, although I tried not to dwell on them. The business with the phones was particularly upsetting. I was sure that from New York City

*Jessi*

to Stoneybrook was a trail of worried people, especially families. As far as I knew, Quint's parents weren't sure where their son was. *My* parents weren't sure where Quint was. They knew where I was, but were they worrying about me? Probably. I wondered if my friends were worried, too. Had Mal or anyone talked to Mama and Daddy? (I also didn't know that the Stoneybrook phones were out of order.) I did know that Mary Anne and Mal were sitting at the Pikes' that night, and I wondered how they were doing, and whether Dawn and her mom had been able to pick up Jeff. What if they couldn't make the trip to the airport? Finally I worried about the parents of all the kids who were stuck here.

"I didn't know you were such a worrier," said Quint as I poured out my thoughts to him. We were sharing my coat, sitting on it in a corner of one of the rehearsal rooms, the wound-up kids running by us.

"I'm not usually," I told him. "But this is an unusual situation. Aren't *you* worried? You haven't even talked to your parents yet."

"I know. But *I'm* safe, so I'm *not* worried. If my parents want to worry, that's their choice. There's nothing I can do about a blizzard. Or about talking to Mom and Dad. And as long as we're in this situation, we should make the best of it. This is kind of fun, don't you think?"

"I don't know about fun, but it's an adventure. That's for sure." I glanced up then and saw Mme Noelle standing in the doorway, surveying the rowdy kids. I caught her eye. When she nodded at me, I stood up. I pulled Quint with me. "I think Mme Noelle wants to speak to us," I said.

We dodged around kids until we were facing my teacher. Ordinarily, I'm shy around Madame, but maybe Quint's presence let me feel a little braver. At any rate, before Mme Noelle had started to speak, I said, "I think the kids are ready to go to sleep — even if *they* don't realize it."

"I sink you are right," agreed Mme Noelle. She looked around uncertainly.

"Do you want me to help you settle them down?" I asked. "I baby-sit all the time. I'm used to it."

"Me, too," said Quint. "I mean, I don't baby-sit, but I'm good at getting my brother and sister to go to sleep."

"Why, sank you, Jessica. Sank you, Queent," said Madame. "Zat would be a beeg help. Zee ozzer teachers and I would appreciate eet."

*Jessi*

Maybe you're wondering where the older kids were. They were in another room, making the most of this night without their parents. They were eating and gossiping and fixing each other's hair. I mean, the girls were. The boys were eating and gossiping and trying to repair this radio that has sat on a table in the office for, like, a hundred years — and never worked.

Quint and I divided the little kids into a group of boys and a group of girls. There were a lot more girls than boys, but that was okay. We weren't creating teams or anything. Then Quint led the boys into one of the changing rooms and I led the girls to another. (A large bathroom is attached to each changing room.) I helped the girls to wash their faces (with paper towels); to brush their teeth (with their fingers, using water); and to take off headbands, jewelry, and anything else that might be uncomfortable to sleep on. They stashed these things in their dance bags and then returned to the practice room. Mme Duprès and Quint and I walked around while the kids arranged their coats on the floor and lay down on them.

"Jessi?" called one of the very youngest girls. "This is not comfy. I have to sleep in my *bed*." Three minutes later she was so sound asleep that she didn't even wake up when the boys, who could not settle down, accidentally kicked a sneaker into the wall beside her during a game of Shoe Hockey (whatever that was).

Eventually, all of the younger kids managed to fall asleep. Quint and I crept out of the room and joined my friends.

"Hey, Jessi," said Katie Beth. "How about a nice cup of . . . soup?"

I groaned. Then I laughed. Katie Beth was teasing. It was only ten-thirty, and already the "good" food (meaning the cookies and the dried fruit) was long gone. Only the instant soup was left. Most of us were starving, but we couldn't face any more of those slimy noodles. Instead we just sat around and talked. Mme Noelle and the other teachers left us alone, which was considerate of them. (Or maybe just smart. I'd heard Mme Duprès say she had a rip-roaring headache.) I talked with the girls; Quint talked with the boys. I would have liked to spend more time with Quint, but once I overheard him say "bowling bag" to this kid, Reed Creason, so I figured they were talking about being guy dancers, which was good for Quint. Anyway, Quint and I had the rest of our visit left for talking — provided his parents let him stay after the night's disaster which, by the way, I thought Quint had handled quite maturely.

The night passed quietly. Holly woke up once after a bad dream, but Mme Duprès helped her to go back to sleep. The older dancers and I slept in one of the other practice rooms, boys on one side, girls on the other — Mme Noelle in the middle.

I woke up at six o'clock with a stiff neck. (I wasn't used to sleeping on my coat, either.) I rolled my head around, trying to loosen the tense muscles. Then I stood up and peered out a window. Day was breaking. The snow was letting up and the sky was cloudy-bright.

By eight o'clock, everyone was up — and the phone was ringing off the hook. The storm was over. Parents would arrive as soon as the roads had been cleared. Quint waited on a phone line to call his parents. They had been worried, needless to say, but not much. They'd thought Quint (and I) were at my house in Stoneybrook. By the time they had realized just how bad the storm had become, the phones in Stoneybrook were already out of order, so they'd assumed Quint was safe but unreachable. (Which was the truth, in any case.)

When the phone calls died down, Mme Noelle announced "Zee coffee shop across zee street eez open, and Mr. Wozneski, zee owner, has agreed to give us free breakfasts. Everybody, put on your coats!"

We ventured outside, Quint holding my hand. The plows had not come through Stamford yet, so we *waded* across the street. By the time we reached the coffee shop, most of us were soaked. But we didn't care. We were Mr. Wozneski's only customers — and we took up nearly every booth. (Quint and I sat by ourselves at a small table.) After a night of instant soup, any food seemed wonderful, and Mr. Wozneski fed us a feast while we dried out.

"This is kind of romantic," I whispered to Quint, as we bit into these bran-and-raisin muffins. (Dawn would have been proud of us.) "Snowbound at dance school, a cozy breakfast at a table for two."

"Yeah," said Quint. "And this is only the beginning. We still have two days together — and the dance tomorrow night."

"I *hope* the dance is still on," I said.

"If it isn't," replied Quint, "it won't matter. You and I will go to some other dance, some other time."

# CHAPTER 20

## Mary Anne

Thursday Morning

Here's what the Pike kids and I ate for breakfast on the day after the blizzard. almost everything in the refrigerator and the cabinets. This may sound like a lot, but it wasn't. Not for nine hungry people. We ate a couple of apples and the ends of two loaves of bread. We ate a package of instant oatmeal. We made tea without milk. Byron ate the last piece of baloney. Adam ate a chicken T.V. dinner....

*Mary anne*

We were scraping bottom. Everyone of us ate *some*thing that morning, but a lot of the food was strange (for breakfast), and Adam was the only one who left the table with a full stomach.

"Maybe," said Margo, "we could cook something new . . ."

"Like what?" I asked. (She was eyeing that box of frosting mix.)

"Spaghetti with chocolate frosting?" she suggested.

"Oh, barf," said Adam.

"Just because you had a chicken dinner — " Nicky began to say.

"The freezer is full of vegetables," Mallory pointed out.

"I'd rather eat Margo's spaghetti," said Jordan.

"My tummy aches," said Claire.

"Uh-oh," I replied.

"It's hungry. It's growling at me."

"Maybe Pizza Express is open now!" cried Mal.

"Oh, good idea." I'd almost gotten used to not having a phone. I realized I could order in food now. So I called Pizza Express. No answer. Then I called Chicken Wings (their ad: Speedy delivery, and service with a fryer).

No answer. I called Tokyo House, even though it didn't open until noon, and even though Margo won't touch Oriental food. No answer. I called Chez Maurice, a fancy French restaurant that had probably never even heard of take-out service. No answer.

After that I phoned Logan.

"I'm hungry," I whined to him, before I said hello or good morning or anything civil. And before I'd asked him how he'd survived the storm.

"I'm sorry," Logan replied. "Where are you? At the Pikes'?"

"Yeah. Mr. and Mrs. Pike got stuck in New York. They didn't come home last night. We're fine, though. Just hungry. There isn't much food left. Did anything interesting happen to you during the blizzard?"

"Nah," said Logan. "Well, except for when the power went out. Mom tried to call the electric company to tell them and then she found out the phone didn't work, either. She was really mad. But then she calmed down and she and Dad and Hunter and Kerry and I played Monopoly by the fireplace."

"Ooh, that sounds cozy," I said. "We didn't think of making a fire."

"We wouldn't have been allowed to make

one," spoke up Mal from across the kitchen. "Not unless the heat had gone off, too."

"What?" said Logan.

"Mal was saying we wouldn't have been allowed to light a fire," I repeated. Then I said, "Guess what. Pizza Express isn't open."

"You're kidding!" exclaimed Logan. "The pizza place is closed at nine o'clock on a morning when we're snowed in and the plows haven't come through yet? What a shock."

I laughed. "Okay, okay. Just remember you're speaking to a person who ate a tiny bowl of instant oatmeal for breakfast."

Byron nudged me. "Can I talk to Logan?" he asked.

"Sure." I handed him the phone.

"Now," said Byron, "you're speaking to a person who ate a single piece of baloney for breakfast."

I don't know what Logan replied, but whatever it was, it made Byron laugh and exclaim, "Oh, gross!" He gave the phone back to me.

"Mary Anne?" said Logan. "You know, I could — "

"Oh!" I cried, interrupting him. "I just remembered something." I was looking out the kitchen window at the back of Stacey's house.

"What's wrong?" asked Logan.

"Nothing. I mean, I don't know if anything is wrong. Last night we tried to call the McGills and there was no answer. This was after dinner, when the storm was really bad. And we didn't see any lights at their house. But then the phones and stuff went out. I should try to call now."

"You should call Dawn, too," said Mal. "See if Jeff got in all right. And tell your dad we're doing okay."

I nodded. "Logan, we should hang up so I can make some calls, okay?"

"Okay. See you later." And then he added softly, "Love you."

" 'Bye," I said. I knew Logan would understand why I hadn't replied, "Love you, too." (The triplets would not have let me hear the end of it.)

I dialed Stacey's number. No one answered. "That's really weird," I said to Mal. "Where could they be? Does it look like they're home?"

"I can't tell," Mal answered, peering out the window. "Are you sure you dialed her number right?"

I was pretty sure, but I dialed it again anyway. No answer.

"Call Dawn," said Mal, frowning.

My dad answered the phone. "At least

186

*you're* home!" I exclaimed. "Can I talk to Dawn, please? Oh, and we're fine, Dad."

"Mary Anne, Dawn isn't here," said my father.

"Oh. Where is she?"

"Still at the airport. Jeff's plane was rerouted to Washington because of the storm, and then the airport closed and Dawn and Sharon were stuck there overnight. I didn't hear from Sharon until a couple of hours ago."

"Oh, Dad!" I exclaimed. "You must have been scared to death." (Sheesh, and I was complaining because I hadn't eaten enough oatmeal that morning.)

"I was pretty nervous," my father agreed. "But I'd heard on the transistor radio that the airport had been closed down, so I was hoping that's where they were. I certainly was relieved when the phone rang this morning."

"I guess so," I said. I was going to tell Dad about Stacey, but before I could, our doorbell rang. "I better go," I said. "Someone's at the door, and half the Pikes aren't dressed yet. I'll call you later. 'Bye!"

"Who's *that*?" yelled Vanessa, dashing upstairs in her nightgown.

"I don't know," I replied. "How could anyone have gotten over here? Nothing's plowed yet. You'd need snowshoes to get around." I peeked out the front window. "Or skis," I added.

You'll never in a million years guess who (what?) was posed in front of the Pikes' front door.

Logan. And his cross-country skis. A knapsack was strapped to his back.

"I come bearing food," said Logan solemnly.

"I don't believe it!" I cried, laughing, as Logan stepped inside.

"Hello, everybody!" he called. "I have food!"

"We're saved!" yelled Margo from her room.

A little while later, the Pike kids (dressed) and Logan and I were crowded around the kitchen table, which was loaded with bananas, peanut butter, bread, crackers, and carrot sticks.

"Real food," said Nicky, sighing with happiness.

"Logan," I said a while later as the younger kids drifted away from the table, "do you think we'll still have the dance tomorrow night?"

"The Winter Wonderland Dance," mur-

mured Mal. "I'd almost forgotten about it. Gosh, I *hope* we have it."

"I wouldn't count on it," said Logan. "Not for tomorrow. That snow is *deep*. Maybe the dance will be postponed until next week."

"It *can't* be postponed!" said Mal. "Ben and I can't wait until next week!"

"Mallory, can we go outside?" yelled Claire.

"Sure," Mal answered. "It's okay, isn't it, Mary Anne? This may be a once-in-a-lifetime experience. What with global warming and all."

The Pike kids put on their layers of outdoor clothes. They spent the morning building a fancy sledding track in the backyard. Then they sailed along it on just about everything except a sled — a saucer, a toboggan, a tray, their stomachs.

At one point, Logan skied over to Stacey's house. He rang the front doorbell. He knocked at their kitchen door. Then he skied back to me.

"No one came to the doors, and their car's gone," he reported.

"That is so weird," I said. "Do you think we should call Claud?"

"What if Claud doesn't know where she is, either?" replied Mallory. "We'll just worry her. Besides, Mrs. McGill is gone, too. I'm sure they're together, wherever they are. They probably just got stuck, like Dawn did."

At that point I became convinced that Stacey and her mom had been in some horrible car accident during the storm. But since I have a reputation as a big worrywart, I kept my mouth closed.

# CHAPTER 21

## Kristy

Thursday Morning

Honestly, sometimes I wish I were a boy. I know there aren't supposed to be big differences between boys and girls, but face it, how many boys do you know who pluck their eyebrows? Or put on makeup? Or curl their hair? Maybe they do if they're actors and they have to get ready for a play or something, but, for instance, I don't see Sam or Charlie doing those things before school every day. And those things take up a lot of time. To top it off, they're boring....

In case you can't tell, I did not exactly appreciate having to get up at the crack of dawn *on a snow day* in order to make myself look great, but that's what I did. I was not about to let Bart catch me with morning breath, sleepy eyes, and bed hair. So when my alarm went off, I tiptoed out of my room and down the hall to the bathroom.

I locked myself in.

Then I rummaged around in the cabinet under the sink.

I had decided that I might as well shave my legs for the first time.

Lucky for me, I found an electric razor *and* the power was back on. I stuck the plug into an outlet. *Bzzzzz* went the razor. I ran it up and down my legs. When I had finished, my legs didn't look much different, although they certainly felt naked. What was the big deal?

I turned my attention to my face and hair. Against my better judgment I took a shower. The pipes in Watson's house (my house) are old and make a lot of noise. An early-morning shower on a snow day would not be appreciated. Oh, well. I did not see that I had a choice.

After my shower, I got out a blow dryer. It's Charlie's, believe it or not, but I didn't think he'd mind if I borrowed it. Then I found an old curling iron. I was about to use it when I decided I could probably electrocute myself since my hair was wet, so first I blew my hair dry and then I curled it. (My hair wound up looking and feeling like limp macaroni. A headband only made things worse.)

Well, on to makeup.

All I own is a leftover tube of mascara and a container of blush, powder form. Even though I wanted to wear eye shadow and stuff, I figured the mascara and blush would be challenging enough. Besides, Mom has all the good makeup, and I couldn't very well sneak through her room and into her bathroom at six A.M. So I had to make do.

When I had finished with the makeup, it looked great. It really did. And I had been in the bathroom for just an hour and a half.

I was no longer the only person up.

Darn. I had not counted on that. From my neck up I looked fantastic. Well, except for my macaroni hair. But below my neck I looked . . . I looked . . . like a person in her nightgown. With naked legs. And I did not want Bart to see that. Frankly, I did not want *any*one to see me, since I had an idea that, all in all, I might appear sort of odd. But as I said, I wasn't the only one up.

I unlocked the bathroom door, planning to listen for a moment, hear nothing but silence, and make a dash for my room. Unfortunately, as soon as I unlocked the door I heard Sam say, "Geez, Kristy, it's about time!"

"What are you doing up?" I hissed.

"I want to enjoy every second of this day off from school," he replied. "How long have you been in there? And what are you doing? You never act like such a girl. I didn't think I'd have to go through this until *Karen* was thirteen."

"By which time you'll be twenty-one and not living here anymore, I hope."

"Very funny."

"Sam, just go back to your room for a sec, please," I said urgently.

"What about me?" said a second voice.

"David Michael?" I asked.

"Yeah. Kristy, I hafta *go*."

"Use your own bathroom," I said. (He and Karen and Andrew and Emily share a bathroom.)

"This one's closer."

"All right." I heaved an enormous sigh. Then I opened the door and strode into the hall. My brothers, each wearing a T-shirt and sweat pants, were leaning against the wall with their arms crossed. When Sam got a look at me, his eyes bugged out. David Michael's mouth dropped open.

"Wrong holiday, Kristy," said Sam. "Christmas is coming, not Halloween."

David Michael didn't say anything. He just ran into the bathroom, laughing.

I don't know who came to the conclusion that women gossip and men don't. My friends and I have learned that this is completely wrong. Women and men both gossip. My brothers are prime examples of male gossipers. By the time everyone was awake and at the breakfast table on Thursday morning, Sam and David Michael had thoroughly spread the word about my appearance when I came out of the bathroom. Every head turned toward me as I slid into my place on the bench. (I noticed that Bart had been seated next to me.)

" 'Morning, honey," said Mom.

"Nice hair," said Sam.

"Nice outfit," said Charlie. (Since I thought I *had* put together a rather nice outfit, I wasn't sure whether Charlie was being serious or sarcastic.)

"Nice makeup," said David Michael, and slapped his hand over his mouth, giggling.

"Hey, Watson, can we install a timer in our bathroom?" asked Sam. "There should be a sixty-minute limit on primping."

He turned to Andrew and said, in his best Mister Rogers voice, "Do you know what *primping* is, Andrew?" (Andrew frowned and shook his head.) "It's making yourself beautiful."

"For your . . . *boyfriend?*" asked Andrew.

"Mom!" I cried.

"Sam!" cried Mom.

"Andrew!" cried Sam.

Andrew glanced around the table. "Emily!" he said finally, and everybody laughed. Even I laughed.

And during the laughter, when no one could hear him, Bart whispered to me, "You look beautiful, Kristy."

I relaxed. "Thanks," I said.

Okay. I had made it. Bart had spent the night at my house. He had survived meals with my family. He had endured teasing by my brothers and sisters. And he hadn't gone away. Emotionally, I mean. He was sitting next to me, telling me I looked beautiful.

If Bart and I could weather that, we could weather anything.

I began to think about something other than myself. The storm, for instance. As soon as breakfast was over I took a good look out the window. I found myself staring at an ocean of snow. It stretched from our front door, across the lawn, across the street, and across another lawn to Shannon Kilbourne's front door. It stretched up and down our road, smooth and rolling, snowdrifts making waves against houses and fences and trees.

Bart stood beside me. "This is the most snow I've ever seen," he said.

"I kind of wish the plows wouldn't come by," I replied. "They'll ruin the view."

"Plus, I won't have any excuse to stay here," added Bart. "I'll have to go home."

"Speaking of home," I said, "I wonder if Jeff got in okay last night. I think I'll call Dawn and Mary Anne." So I did. "Well, for heaven's sake," I said to Bart when I'd hung up the phone. "Guess what. Neither Mary Anne nor Dawn was there. Mary Anne is still at the Pikes' because Mr. and Mrs. Pike got stuck in New York. And Dawn is still at the airport! I didn't hear anything about people stranded at the airport on the news this morning. Just that the power's back on, the phones are working again, and what the current temperature is. I hope the newspaper has better stories." Then it occurred to me to call the rest of my friends. Only Mallory was at home. She and Mary Anne were staying at her house until her parents returned.

"Call Stacey," Mal said. "No one's been able to reach her or her mom."

I dialed the McGills'. No answer.

So I called Claudia. Mr. Kishi answered Claud's phone. "She's still at the Perkinses'," he told me. "They couldn't get home last night."

Wow. Pretty interesting. Before I called Claud at the Perkinses', I decided to phone Jessi. I wondered what sort of story she had.

"Jessi got stuck at dance school!" Becca told me excitedly. "Daddy couldn't pick her up. She ate breakfast at a *restaurant* this morning. Quint, too. He's with her. Mama and Daddy can't get them until the plows come."

I phoned Claud right away. "Do you have any idea what *hap*pened to the BSC last night?" I exclaimed. "Somebody should write about us. Hey, where's Stacey? Mal's all worried because Stace and her mom aren't home."

"They aren't home?" Claud repeated. "That's weird. Stacey called me yesterday afternoon. She wanted me to come to the mall with her because she was getting her hair permed. I know she didn't have plans last night. She and her mom were supposed to be at home. I wonder where they could be."

I wondered, too.

And I began to worry.

# Dawn

Wednesday Night
and Thursday Morning
I tried to sleep Wednesday
night. I really did. I read and
read and read. I was sure that
at some point I'd begin to nod
off. I don't know how Mom slept.
But she did. So did a lot of other
people. Not Carter, though. I met
Carter at about three in the
morning. At first, he scared me
to death....

I think that if I'd been much younger I would have spent Wednesday night saying to my mother, "Now what time is it? . . . *Now* what time is it?" However, I was wearing a watch, so I just kept looking at it. I bet I checked it every two minutes. Nine thirty-three, nine thirty-five, nine thirty-seven, nine thirty-nine.

"Honey," said Mom after awhile, "looking at your watch isn't going to make the time pass any more quickly."

I sighed. "I know. It's like drivers who think they can clear up traffic jams by blasting their horns. The two things are not connected."

Mom smiled at me. "Can't you concentrate on your book?"

"Not really. And the book is good. I just keep thinking about Jeff. I wonder if he knows why we aren't calling him."

"He probably does," my mother replied. "When nobody in Washington can reach anyone here, they'll figure it out. Also, maybe Jeff has spoken to Richard. I'm sure Jeff tried to call the house."

"Oh, yeah," I said, brightening. "Sure."

"Feel better?"

"Yup."

"Ready to sleep?"

"Nope. But maybe I can read now."

"Okay. Listen, I'm sure the airport is safe, but don't, you know, go wandering around during the night without me. Let me know if you want to go to the restroom or the snack bar. I'll come with you."

Ordinarily, I might have thought Mom was being unreasonably overprotective, but not that night. I glanced at the empty corridors, at the frustrated and tired people around me, and I shivered.

"No problem," I said to Mom. "Um, are you going to sleep now?"

"I might take a little nap," she answered.

"Let's go to the bathroom first."

So we did. When we returned to our seats, Mom didn't just nap, she fell into this deep sleep.

I sat up with my book. I tried different positions. I flung my legs over the armrest. The armrest hurt the backs of my knees. I curled them into a ball, but couldn't find a good place for my head. I tried Mom's position, sitting up straight. She looked like she was at a fancy restaurant, waiting to be served dinner. But her eyes were closed. Also, she was snoring.

I hoped no one would hear. Or if they did hear, that they wouldn't realize the sounds were coming from my mother. Then I hoped they wouldn't think *I* was snoring. I made a big show of looking awake.

At midnight I asked the woman behind the desk when she thought Jeff's plane would arrive.

"Around seven, maybe," she replied.

At two o'clock, she went off duty. A man took her place. I asked *him* when Jeff's plane would arrive.

"Probably before noon," he answered. (Some help.)

I returned to my seat. I snuggled against my coat. I closed my eyes. Then I opened them. I looked at the other people trying to sleep. Across from me was an older couple. In another row was an entire family — a mom, a dad, and three little boys. A bunch of people seemed to be traveling by themselves.

My eyes started to droop. In all honesty, I do not think I fell asleep, though. *Maybe* I did, but I doubt it. Anyway, a while later I was lolling in the chair, my eyes closed, remembering what Mom had said earlier about the airport and whether it was safe, when I became certain that someone was standing silently behind me, staring. I was trying to decide whether turning around and opening my eyes would be foolish, when I felt a hand on mine.

I nearly shrieked.

I knew it wasn't Mom's hand. She hadn't stirred.

"Ah-ma-*mah!*" crowed a little voice. A baby's?

Sure enough, when I did find the courage to turn around, I was looking into a pair of deep black eyes, which gazed seriously at me from a brown face. After a moment, the cheeks dimpled into a smile.

"Hello, there," I whispered. "Where did you come from?" Then I recognized the boy as one of the kids in the family I'd noticed earlier. I sat up and looked for them. There were his brothers and his mother, sound asleep. But where was his father?

"Carter!" called a panicky voice.

*There* was the father. He was running through the corridor, carrying a diaper bag. I got to my feet and picked up the baby. "Is this who you're looking for?" I asked the man.

"Carter! Thank heavens!" he said, reaching for the baby. "Where did you find him?" he asked me.

"Right here. I just opened my eyes and here he was."

The man shook his head, smiling. "Carter

is our little night owl," he said. "He just won't sleep. He wants to stay up and play. I decided to walk him to the restroom so I could change him, and . . . I don't know. How can such short legs move so quickly? I wish he would drop off for awhile."

Carter's dad and I chatted until Carter actually did drop off. By then, even I was feeling drowsy, and finally I managed to doze, my head resting on Mom's shoulder. The doze turned into a sleep.

The next thing I knew, it was nearly seven-thirty. I opened my eyes to a bustling airport (bustling compared to the middle of the night) and a glaringly white world.

"Good morning, sleepyhead," teased my mother.

"Sleepyhead! I didn't fall asleep until, like, four o'clock. I feel as if I've been to a sleep-over — on a school night. When's Jeff going to be here? Is he already on his way? Hey, I'm hungry!"

"Let's eat breakfast, then," said Mom, "and I'll tell you what's been happening." She stood up, closing her book.

"I must look awful," I said, yawning. "Just what I always wanted. To wake up with fifty other people."

"Well, *no*body here is a raving beauty," said

Mom. "Not at this hour after a night in a waiting room."

Mom and I went to the snack bar for breakfast. I told her about Carter, and she gave me a blizzard/airport update: The storm was over. Twenty-five inches of snow had fallen at the airport. The airport was in the process of reopening. Jeff was due to arrive around 11:15. The phones worked. Mom had spoken to Richard. Richard had *not* spoken to Jeff, since both the electricity and the phones had been out in Stoneybrook the night before. Mom had tried to call Jeff in Washington that morning, had not been able to reach him (he was traveling, with his personal flight attendant, from the hotel to the airport), but she had spoken to another flight attendant, who said that Jeff *was* upset, but at least he was all in one piece.

After breakfast, Mom and I waited. I went to the restroom and tried to wash up and make myself look presentable. I watched snowplows clear the runways. I played with Carter and his brothers.

At 11:15, Mom and I were among a crowd of people pressed against the windows, watching the arrival of the plane that should have arrived about fifteen hours earlier. Everyone cheered as the plane touched down. Then we moved to the gate, to greet the passengers as they left the plane. Jeff (with his flight attendant) was one of the first people to enter the terminal. When he and Mom and I spotted each other, all three of us burst into tears.

Jeff hugged Mom and wouldn't let go of her. "I thought I would never get here," he said. "I thought I would never see you."

"We were worried," Mom replied, sniffling. "We tried to call, but we couldn't reach you. Everyone kept saying you were all right, though. The phones stopped working. We couldn't call you or Richard or anyone."

"Mom and I spent the night in the airport," I announced.

"Really?" said Jeff. "You waited for me all this time?"

"Of course!" exclaimed Mom. Then she added, "What an adventure you've had. Was the hotel nice?"

Jeff perked up. "I got to order room service!" he exclaimed, as Mom and I put on our coats and the three of us headed for the baggage claim. "They said I could order whatever I wanted for breakfast. So I had toast and hash browns and French fries."

"Very well-balanced," I commented.

The more Jeff talked, the happier he sounded. He even sounded *proud*. After we

had found his suitcase and were walking toward the car, he said, "You know, I wasn't the only kid traveling alone. There was this little girl. She was only eight." (Jeff is only ten.) "And she just kept crying. She thought we'd been hijacked! And while we were circling around and around she got airsick. You know what was in my hotel room?" Jeff went on.

"What?" said Mom and I. We had found our car and were unlocking it and loading in Jeff's suitcase.

"A shoehorn. And I was allowed to *keep* it. It's in my suitcase. I'm going to give it to Richard for Christmas. In his stocking."

Jeff chattered all the way to Stoneybrook. As we turned onto our street, he exclaimed, "You know, last night wasn't so bad after all!"

A few minutes later, we had a happy reunion with Richard. Then he said, "Dawn, Mary Anne wants you to call her. She's at the Pikes'."

I dialed Mal's number, and Mary Anne answered the phone. "Dawn! I'm so glad you're back!" she cried. "But guess what. Stacey and her mother are missing!"

# CHAPTER 23

## Stacey

Wednesday Evening
and Thursday Morning

Doo-dee, doo-doo, doo-dee, doo-doo. I was in a scene from a <u>Twilight Zone</u> show. My mom and I were lost on a lonely dark road at nighttime during a snowstorm, and suddenly...

The man was looming in the window of our car. (Actually, he seemed quite concerned, but I didn't think about that until later.) And Mom was looking at me, waiting for me to say, "Why, I think climbing into a car with a strange man is a *won*derful idea!"

We *were* in a pretty tight spot, though. I mean, without the man. We really didn't know where we were, we were stuck in a car without heat in the middle of a raging blizzard, and I was famished. I guess you have to take a chance and trust people *some*times. Anyway, I was with Mom.

I nodded my head. "Okay," I whispered.

Mom turned to the man. "Thank you," she said. "We'd love to go home with you. I don't know what would have happened if you hadn't come along. You must be a miracle."

The man grinned. "I'm Ken Schiavone," he said as Mom and I climbed out of our car. (We locked the doors and just left the car sitting by the side of the road, half buried in snow.)

"I'm Maureen McGill," said Mom, "and this is my daughter, Stacey. We live in Stoney-brook. We were on our way home from the Washington Mall."

Mr. Schiavone held the doors to his car open

for Mom and me and we slid in, Mom in front, me in back.

"I wasn't sure I was going to get home myself," said Mr. Schiavone, as he urged his car forward. "I haven't seen weather like this in years."

"Where did you say you live?" I asked. "At the end of the road?"

"Not quite the end," Mr. Schiavone replied. "But further down the road. My wife and I moved in last year. We bought a Victorian monstrosity. Six months ago we had our first baby," he added proudly. "Mason. He's something of a monstrosity himself."

"You have a baby?" I repeated.

Mom turned around and smiled at me. Then she said to Mr. Schiavone, "Stacey loves children. She's a wonderful baby-sitter."

"That's terrific. I'm sure Mason will be glad to see a new face." Mr. Schiavone nosed the car into a dark turnoff. I couldn't see anything. No house, no lights. I could barely make out the drive we were traveling on.

This is it, I thought. He's taking us deep into the woods, and Mom and I will never be seen alive again. We'll wind up as a story in one of those books about missing people and strange disappearances.

I was working myself into a pretty good panic when suddenly a beautiful house appeared through the snow, as if by magic. It looked like a house from a fairy tale, lit inside and out, a green wreath with a plaid ribbon hanging on the door, the gold lights on a Christmas tree twinkling through a window.

"Ooh," I said, as Mr. Schiavone pulled into the garage. "This is beautiful."

"Thank you. I must confess, my wife and I are Christmas nuts. We put up the decorations about a week ago. We like to enjoy a long Christmas."

"That's nice," said Mom. "Stace, maybe you and I should have an old-fashioned Christmas this year."

"Maybe," I replied. That Christmas would be my first as a divorced kid, and I wasn't sure how I felt about the holiday.

Mom and I followed Mr. Schiavone into his house, through the kitchen, and to the living room, another fairy-tale sight. There was the tree I had seen from outside. Stacks of presents were already piled under it. A fire was blazing in the fireplace, and on the chimney above had been hung another wreath, similar to the one on the door, but twice its size. And sitting in an armchair was Mrs. Schiavone, who was reading a story to Mason. What was she reading? *The Night Before Christmas*, of course.

Mrs. Schiavone looked up in surprise when Mom and I trailed into the living room after Mr. Schiavone.

"Hi, honey. I brought us a couple of visitors for the night. They were stuck a little ways down the road," said Mr. Schiavone.

"Our car died," Mom added apologetically. "We were stranded."

Mrs. Schiavone stood up, shifting Mason to her hip. "My goodness," she said. "Here. Take off your wet things. Dry out by the fireplace. I'll add two plates to the table. . . . Where do you live?"

The adults introduced themselves again, and Mom told Mrs. Schiavone our story. "I guess there's no point in calling Triple A," she said. "Not at this hour, in this weather."

"Of course not," agreed Mrs. Schiavone. "Please. Spend the night here. You can call Triple A first thing in the morning. Is there anyone you need to call now? Your husband?"

"No, no," said Mom quickly. "We're divorced. It's just Stacey and me. I don't think we need to make any calls. But . . ."

"Yes?" prompted Mrs. Schiavone.

"Stacey's diabetic."

"No sugar for me," I interrupted, "and I need to give myself some insulin."

215

Mrs. Schiavone was great. She showed me to the bathroom. As soon as I came out, she handed Mason to me and hurried into the kitchen, followed by Mom, saying, "Just tell me what Stacey can eat. We have plenty of food here."

I sat by the fire, holding Mason and becoming very aware of the smell of my new perm. Mason noticed it, too, I think. He kept wrinkling his nose. But when I picked up *The Night Before Christmas* and began to read to him again, he settled down. "You like stories, Mason?" I asked.

"He loves to be read to," said Mr. Schiavone from across the room. "We've been reading to him since the day he came home from the hospital."

Hmm. Good information. I stored it away, planning to mention it at the next BSC meeting. *Even little babies like to be read to.*

Considering that the evening had started out to be so frightening, it sure ended nicely. The Schiavones and Mom and I had a great time together. Mr. and Mrs. Schiavone were . . . wonderful. Funny, warm, matter-of-fact (my diabetes didn't faze them a bit; they just asked what I could eat and then fixed it for me), understanding (no more questions about Dad or the divorce), interesting, outgoing, involved, creative, you name it. And Mason was charming. The Schiavones let me put him to bed. I wished they lived closer to Stoneybrook so we could be friends and I could sit for Mason.

By the next day, Mom and I almost didn't want to leave, and the Schiavones seemed reluctant to say good-bye. So we hung around together, postponing calling Triple A, using the snow as an excuse. And it *was* a pretty good excuse. Mr. Schiavone leaned out the front door on Thursday morning and stuck a yardstick in the snow. All but six inches were covered. Two and a half feet had fallen.

"Treasure this," Mom told me. "You may not see the likes of it again."

The morning passed, the sun came out, and finally the snowplows cleared even the back country roads. Mom had no more reasons for not calling Triple A. By one o'clock, we were on our way home.

We took the highway.

I insisted.

"The snow's awfully pretty, isn't it?" said Mom.

"Now that the sun is shining, the road's been plowed, the car works, and we know where we're going," I answered.

Mom laughed. She drove home slowly. It

was nearly two o'clock when we finally reached our street. To my surprise, I saw Claudia standing on the front porch of our house. When we pulled up in the street (our driveway wasn't shoveled, of course), she bolted across the snowy yard and threw her arms around me as I climbed out of the car.

"Oh, my lord!" she cried. "You're safe! You're alive!"

Now, how did Claud know that a stranger had picked us up and given us a ride to his house deep in the woods?

"Where *were* you guys?" exclaimed Claudia. "Have you really been gone since yesterday? You scared us to death!"

I looked at Mom, then back at Claud. "I didn't think anyone would even realize we weren't at home," I said.

"We weren't sure until this morning," Claud told me. "Yesterday Mal and Mary Anne didn't see any lights at your house, and they couldn't get you on the phone. But then the power went out and the phones went out so we couldn't tell whether you'd come home later or not. But when we couldn't reach you to*day* we panicked."

"I'm sorry," I said, as Claud walked Mom and me to the front door. "But what's wrong? Why were you trying to get hold of us?"

"We just wanted to know if you were all right. You wouldn't believe what happened to everyone last night. Jessi got stuck in Stamford and spent the night at her dance school; the Perkinses couldn't come home, so I spent the night with Myriah and Gabbie and Laura; Dawn and her mom spent the night at the *air*port . . ."

Claudia went on and on. She listened to my story. Then she said, "I better call Kristy. She'll want to know this." So she called her, and a few moments later she was saying, "What? You're kidding?! I'll spread the word!" When she hung up she said to me, "School will be open tomorrow, and the dance is still on. Kristy just talked to that kid she knows — the one whose mother is on the school board. We were afraid the dance would be called off because of the snow."

Claud phoned the other BSC members, and before I knew it, the entire club had gathered at my house. Logan and Quint, too.

"Don't ever think we wouldn't miss you," Claud said to me.

"Yeah. I'm very nosy," added Mal. "I can usually tell whether you're home or not, and it matters to me."

"Okay, okay. I'll stay in touch!" I said. "That's a promise."

*Stacey*

Then we went outside. We built a mammoth snowman and snow woman in our front yard.

"Look. They're ready for the Winter Wonderland Dance," whispered Mary Anne. "Just like we are."

"Tomorrow night is going to be magic," I said.

"But most important," added Kristy, "the BSC will be there *together*."

## EPILOGUE

### *Kristy*

"OH! oh, my — Mom! Hey, Mom!"

"Kristy, what on earth is going on?" asked my mother.

"Mom, you'll never guess who was on the phone. That was Marian Tan, the woman from the *Stoneybrook News.* I mean, the editor. And she wants to print my article. Honest. She really likes the idea. And she's going to *pay* me."

"That's fantastic, honey," said Mom.

"Boy, I have to get to work."

"Didn't your friends already write about their blizzard experiences?" Mom wanted to know.

"Yes, but there's too much material for one newspaper article. I have to trim it down. And make it fit together. Plus, we're all still working on our final entries — you know, how things ended up, what happened after the storm, how the Winter Wonderland Dance went. That kind of thing."

I was pretty sure that a phone call saying "SNOWBOUND!" was going to be published would bring in those last pieces of material quickly. And I was right. By the next day, I had everything I needed for the article:

*You aren't really going to publish this stuff, are you, Kristy? The stuff about Logan and me and the dance? What does that have to do with the blizzard? Well, I suppose it is sort of connected. Anyway, so Logan stayed at the Pikes' with Mal and me until Mr. and Mrs. Pike returned from New York. His food came in very handy, since we ate it for lunch, too. I'm not quite so glad he skied over, though. In the afternoon, Adam tried to use the skis and nearly killed himself.*

*The dance on Friday was wonderful. It was dreamy.*

Kristy, you don't want all the details, do you? They're private. Logan and I had fun, that's all.

*MaryAnne*


Jeff seems to be over his ordeal. I think Mom and I are, too. The three of us took lo-o-o-o-ng naps when we got home from the airport. Somehow, the plows cleared almost all the roads in Stoneybrook by Thursday night. So school was open on Friday. And the dance was held. Price Irving and I went as planned. You know something? Remember how I had that enormous crush on Price? Well, I nearly forgot about him (and the dance) when I was so concerned about Jeff. Maybe Price isn't as important to me as I had thought. Who knows? Anyway, we had a good time.

*Dawn*

*Kristy*

Maria and Gabie had so much fun playing outdoors on Thursday. They bilt the snow family they had talked abuot and they made snowballs and snow angles and pulled each other around on the sled. Rigth before lunchtime, Jamie Newton and some other kids came over to play. I had to stay inside with Laura, but I kept an eye on the kids though the kichen window.

Mr. and Mrs. Perkins came home not long after Jamie came over. You shold have see the greeting Mariah and gabby gave their parnets. It was grate. They hugged them and hugged them.

Iri and I had a grate time at the dance I think mabe I like him beter than just a freind!

*Claudia*

Heaven. I'm in heaven. The dance was wonderful. Quint is wonderful. Life is wonderful.

*Jessi*

224

Mom and Dad got home in the nick of time. Mary Anne and I had reached the end of our rope. We were tired of crackers, tired of complaints, and tired of hearing about the Abominable Snowman. We were even tired of snow itself. If the storm had canceled the dance, I would have... Well, I'm not sure what I would have done, but it would have been drastic. Luckily, the dance was held after all. I am not the world's best dancer, but Ben doesn't care, which is one reason I like him. Now I can't wait for the Valentine's Day Dance.

*Mallory*

I'm still sorry for giving you guys such a scare.

It's funny, but some good things came from the awful experience Mom and I had. One, we got to know the Schiavones. As soon as we came home, Mom mailed a Christmas card to them, and today we got one back, with a picture of Mason. Mom is going to invite the Schiavones to dinner some time in January.

Two, Mom and I are closer. She was impressed to see that I really do keep my insulin injection kit with me at all

Kristy

times. And in a backward sort of way, I was almost relieved to see Mom get scared on Wednesday night. It is nice to know that parents are not perfect.

Three, even though we made you guys worry, it was kind of nice for Mom and me to realize just how much you care about us.

Let me see. The dance was okay, but someone should tell Austin that since he does not yet shave, he should not wear after-shave lotion. By the way, my perm looked fantastic, but I'm not sure it was worth getting stranded in a snowstorm.

Stacey

The dance was awesome. Bart and I had so much fun. We didn't actually dance very much, but we hung around with Mary Anne and Logan and Jessi and Quint and everyone. Bart showed the boys how to turn their eyelids inside out. Somehow, this did not seem immature. Just fun.

I applied my own makeup before the dance, and Bart told me (again) that I looked beautiful.

226

I hope I did. This time, I spent nearly two hours primping in the bathroom. Also, I bought Bart a blue carnation and he bought me an orchid corsage!

I guess I better go. I have to call Bart. He's going to come over and help me write the newspaper article.

Kristy

Oh, Karen wants to add something here:

EMILY JUNIOR IS BACK. DARN OLD DAVID MICHAEL RATNAPPED HER.

AND WE ALL LIVED HAPPILY EVER AFTER.

THE END

## About the Author

ANN M. MARTIN did *a lot* of baby-sitting when she was growing up in Princeton, New Jersey. She is a former editor of books for children, and was graduated from Smith College.

Ms. Martin lives in New York City with her cats, Mouse and Rosie. She likes ice cream and *I Love Lucy*; and she hates to cook.

Ann Martin's Apple Paperbacks include *Yours Turly, Shirley; Ten Kids, No Pets; With You and Without You; Bummer Summer*; and all the other books in the Baby-sitters Club series.

# THE BABY-SITTERS CLUB®

## by Ann M. Martin

The Baby-sitters' business is booming, and the fun never stops!
Don't miss out on any of it—collect them all!

*More titles...* ▶

*The Baby-sitters Club titles continued...*

| | | |
|---|---|---|
| ❏ MG42497-1 | #31 Dawn's Wicked Stepsister | $2.95 |
| ❏ MG42496-3 | #32 Kristy and the Secret of Susan | $2.95 |
| ❏ MG42495-5 | #33 Claudia and the Great Search | $2.95 |
| ❏ MG42494-7 | #34 Mary Anne and Too Many Boys | $2.95 |
| ❏ MG42508-0 | #35 Stacey and the Mystery of Stoneybrook | $2.95 |
| ❏ MG43565-5 | #36 Jessi's Baby-sitter | $2.95 |
| ❏ MG43566-3 | #37 Dawn and the Older Boy | $2.95 |
| ❏ MG43567-1 | #38 Kristy's Mystery Admirer | $2.95 |
| ❏ MG43568-X | #39 Poor Mallory! | $2.95 |
| ❏ MG44082-9 | #40 Claudia and the Middle School Mystery | $2.95 |
| ❏ MG43570-1 | #41 Mary Anne Versus Logan | $2.95 |
| ❏ MG44083-7 | #42 Jessi and the Dance School Phantom | $2.95 |
| ❏ MG43572-8 | #43 Stacey's Emergency | $2.95 |
| ❏ MG43573-6 | #44 Dawn and the Big Sleepover | $2.95 |
| ❏ MG43574-4 | #45 Kristy and the Baby Parade | $3.25 |
| ❏ MG43569-8 | #46 Mary Anne Misses Logan | $3.25 |
| ❏ MG44971-0 | #47 Mallory on Strike | $3.25 |
| ❏ MG43571-X | #48 Jessi's Wish | $3.25 |
| ❏ MG44970-2 | #49 Claudia and the Genius of Elm Street | $3.25 |
| ❏ MG44240-6 | Baby-sitters on Board! Super Special #1 | $3.50 |
| ❏ MG44239-2 | Baby-sitters Summer Vacation Super Special #2 | $3.50 |
| ❏ MG43973-1 | Baby-sitters Winter Vacation Super Special #3 | $3.50 |
| ❏ MG42493-9 | Baby-sitters Island Adventure Super Special #4 | $3.50 |
| ❏ MG43575-2 | California Girls! Super Special #5 | $3.50 |
| ❏ MG43576-0 | New York, New York! Super Special #6 | $3.50 |
| ❏ MG44963-X | Snowbound Super Special #7 | $3.50 |

**Available wherever you buy books...or use this order form.**

Scholastic Inc., P.O. Box 7502, 2931 E. McCarty Street, Jefferson City, MO 65102

Please send me the books I have checked above. I am enclosing $_____
(please add $2.00 to cover shipping and handling). Send check or money order - no cash or C.O.D.s please.

Name _____

Address _____

City_____ State/Zip _____

Please allow four to six weeks for delivery. Offer good in the U.S. only. Sorry, mail orders are not available to residents of Canada. Prices subject to change.

BSC591

# Who Would You Like to be Snowbound With?

## Tell us and win your very own

## Snowbound Kit!

### 100 Winners Receive a Snowbound Kit filled with BABY-SITTERS CLUB stuff!

- Backpack • Sleeping Bag • Nightshirt
- Videos • Board Game

When a massive blizzard hits Stoneybrook, the Baby-sitters are all snowed in...but at least they aren't alone! What about you? If you were snowed in, who is the *one person* you would want to be with you? A parent? Your best friend? A movie star? Let us know and you may win an official Baby-sitters Club Snowbound Kit! Just fill in the coupon below and return it by March 31, 1992.

**Rules:** Entries must be postmarked by March 31, 1992. Winners will be picked at random and notified by mail. No purchase necessary. Valid only in the U.S and Canada. Void where prohibited. Taxes on prizes are the responsibility of the winners and their immediate families. Employees of Scholastic Inc.; its agencies, affiliates, subsidiaries; and their immediate families not eligible. For a complete list of winners, send a self-addressed stamped envelope to: The Baby-sitters Club Snowbound Giveaway, Winners List, at the address provided below.

Fill in the coupon below or write the information on a 3" x 5" piece of paper and mail to: **THE BABY-SITTERS CLUB SNOWBOUND GIVEAWAY**, P.O. Box 7500, Jefferson City, MO 65102. Canadian residents send entries to: Iris Ferguson, Scholastic Inc., 123 Newkirk Road, Richmond Hill, Ontario, Canada L4C365.

- - - - - - - - - - - - - - - - - - - - - - - - - - - - - - - - - - - - - - - - - - - - - - - - - - - -

### The Baby-sitters Club Snowbound Giveaway

Who would you like to be snowbound with? _____

Why? _____

Name_____ Age_____

Street _____

City _____State/Zip_____

#### Where did you buy this Baby-sitters Club book?
- ☐ Bookstore      ☐ Drugstore      ☐ Supermarket      ☐ Book Club
- ☐ Book Fair      ☐ Other_____(specify)

BSC691